SOLID GROUND

SOLID GROUND

AN ADAIRSVILLE HERITAGE MYSTERY
BOOK 1

Danny & Wanda Pelfrey

CrossLink Publishing

CrossLink Publishing
1601 Mt. Rushmore Rd, STE 3288
Rapid City, SD 57702

Ordering Information:
Quantity sales. Special discounts are available on quantity purchases by corporations, associations, and others. For details, contact the "Special Sales Department" at the address above.

Solid Ground/Pelfrey —1st ed.

ISBN 978-1-63357-308-6

Library of Congress Control Number: 2020933688

First edition: 10 9 8 7 6 5 4 3 2 1

Contents

CHAPTER 1 1

CHAPTER 2 11

CHAPTER 3 21

CHAPTER 4 31

CHAPTER 5 39

CHAPTER 6 49

CHAPTER 7 59

CHAPTER 8 69

CHAPTER 9 79

CHAPTER 10 89

CHAPTER 11..99

CHAPTER 12.. 107

CHAPTER 13.. 117

CHAPTER 14.. 127

CHAPTER 15.. 137

CHAPTER 16.. 147

CHAPTER 17.. 156

CHAPTER 18.. 165

CHAPTER 19.. 175

CHAPTER 20.. 185

CHAPTER 21 195

CHAPTER 22 205

CHAPTER 23 215

CHAPTER 24 221

AFTERWORD 229

CHAPTER 1

The two boys in the tent only a couple of hundred feet from the Boyd Mountain Road were surprised to hear cars. It was after one o'clock in the morning. There was rarely any traffic on the road at this hour. When the two cars came to a halt, the middle schoolers crawled out of their small tent and squatted behind some bushes. They were close enough to vaguely see and hear the drivers who came out of the cars on the opposite side of the road.

"Let's get him behind the wheel," one of the men directed. Because the dome lights in the lead car came on when the driver's side door was opened, the boys could see what looked like an unconscious person being put behind the wheel. "Now, make sure it's out of park in drive and turn the steering wheel so the car will make it past the closest trees and roll awhile before crashing." With the car's engine still humming, one of the men slammed the car door and pushed the car from that spot. The other pushed from behind. The car rolled at least sixty feet before it slammed into a tree.

"You don't think they'll figure out the car was pushed off the road, do you?" The voice was that of the second man—one the boys had not heard till now.

"This is Adairsville. Gibbs don't live here and there's no NCIS. Our boys will never figure it out."

The two men got into the other car and drove toward the bottom of the mountain.

"Do you think we should go down there and check on that man?" one of the boys asked.

"I think we should pack up and get as far away from this spot as we can," his friend answered. "My dad always says it's a good thing for a man to mind his own business."

His shaken friend did not object to that plan.

****

Riley was almost always restless when sleeping in an unfamiliar environment. The setting in which she now found herself was certainly one to which she was unaccustomed. It was also somewhat bizarre. Even though she grew up in a parsonage as the daughter of a pastor, before last evening, she had never spent a full night in a church. It wasn't exactly a church, but it had been once. Uncle James, who always fancied the atypical, had managed to do an incredible job in transforming the little hundred-year-old white church building into a lovely residence. He and a white-headed couple, Amos and Carol Edwards, had lived there for several months before his untimely death.

Having slept little the previous night, Riley crashed well before eleven. It didn't take long to fall asleep, but now she could see by looking at the clock beside her bed that it was just past two o'clock. A couple of minutes earlier she was awakened by what sounded like voices coming from a distance. Now wide awake, Riley continued to lie in the soft bed. She turned her slim body toward the west wall, the side from which she thought the sound originated and propped on her elbow with her chin and cheek resting in her right hand. She listened but heard nothing. *Maybe the voices came from my dreams or from Amos and Carol in their residence across the hallway.* Nevertheless, after a couple of minutes, the curious twenty-two-year-old recent college graduate got to her feet to pull back the curtains and look outside.

At first, she saw nothing from her perch on the second floor of what was once part of the Sunday school building. Now it was a beautiful little efficiency apartment. She raised her head to look several hundred yards to the hillside where she, a few hours earlier, had walked through the maze of tombstones. She saw a moving light that was visible for a few seconds before disappearing into the wooded area behind the cemetery. *Probably kids out when they should be home in bed,* she decided. *Some parents need to do a better job of supervising their children,* Riley, now irritated at being awakened, told herself. *I'll be a whole lot more comfortable when Kirby gets here tomorrow. It'll be good to see him. It's been two months since we were last together at Uncle James's funeral.* Now unable to go back to sleep, Riley thought about how close she had been with her older brother in her early and middle teens. A withdrawn disposition probably brought on by a series of brutal setbacks in Kirby's personal life was the culprit that had robbed them of much of that closeness. That, along with circumstances that kept them separated by hundreds of miles. Riley had learned to be reasonably independent. The turns her life had taken demanded that, but she needed her brother. She hoped two or three weeks together in the little Georgia town of Adairsville, where their father had spent his childhood, would help restore life to their relationship.

Riley spent the next two hours tossing and turning while her mind went from one extreme to the other reviewing the ups and downs of her life over the past few years. The downs seemed to always go disastrously deep, such as the loss of both parents in one tragic accident. On the other hand, she had experienced some wonderful high points. She cherished those. *The good and the bad,* she thought. *All part of life.* Finally, she dozed, but sleep came and went throughout the remainder of the night. She arose at six thirty to shower and make herself presentable for breakfast with Amos and Carol.

****

"After spending the day with her yesterday, what do you think of Riley?" Amos asked his wife as he took two pieces of toast from the toaster and replaced them with two more slices of bread. "Is she, indeed, the young lady she seems to be?"

"I've seen no reason to believe otherwise," Carol answered. "I've a feeling she's as beautiful on the inside as on the outside. She seems to be everything her Uncle James always bragged she was. She's a mature young lady for her twenty-two years."

"I guess she has had to grow up fast. How old was she when her parents were killed in that plane crash?"

"She told me she had turned eighteen two months before it happened. I'd forgotten they were returning from a mission trip in Haiti. She was six weeks away from starting college. Being pretty much on her own since then, she's done remarkably well. I had to press her hard to get her to tell me her grade point average. I think I would've been anxious to announce it to the world if I'd completed my pre-law degree at Boston College with a three point nine. She chose to go to Emory Law School because it's near to here and it's reasonably close to her brother in St Petersburg. She probably could've chosen just about any law school in the country, including those snooty eastern schools."

"I hope we have enough here in our little town to keep her entertained this summer," Amos remarked.

"Oh, I think she'll fall in love with Adairsville, and the people of Adairsville are certain to love her. She's not the type that has to be entertained. It's her brother I worry about, but, if I understand correctly, he's only going to be with us for two or three weeks."

"I don't know if he's going to be able to take care of all the business he will have as the executor of his uncle's estate in that short time period. You know as well as I that James was never able to pass up a good investment. I wonder if those two know how well off they are." Amos laughed.

"He did all right by us as well," Carol said with a smile.

"He was a good friend. The twenty-one years we spent with him were great years," Amos spoke reflectively.

When Carol heard the doorbell, she walked from the kitchen through a small dining area into their living room to open the door. "Come on in, Riley. You tell me how you like your eggs and breakfast will be ready in five minutes."

"I've always eaten my eggs scrambled," Riley told her host. "I hope you haven't gone to a lot of trouble for me. I'm not much of a breakfast person. I tend to nibble mornings and at lunch and then eat more than I should at dinner."

"Looking at you, honey, I can't imagine you ever overeating. Now, me, that's another story. I enjoy three full meals a day, and it shows. I haven't been your size since I was . . . actually, I've never been your size, not as an adult."

"Size has never bothered me. My friends, through the years, have come in a variety of sizes. Throughout my childhood I was usually the tallest person in my class. That bothered me until I discovered a lot of advantages to being tall. I'm proud of every inch of my current almost five-eleven frame."

"I'm sure you've never been told that you're a beautiful young lady." Carol smiled at her guest. "I've no doubt you could be one of those famous New York supermodels if you wanted to."

"Oh Carol, I can't see getting much satisfaction in life from walking across a runway with a lot of people watching, even if I were attractive enough to pull it off," Riley responded.

"How long were you with Uncle James, Mr. Edwards?" Riley asked a few minutes later while putting a dab of Carol's home-made peach preserves on her toast.

"Please, Riley, call me Amos. I know you're being the polite lady you were raised to be, but I want us to be good friends, and friends call each other by first names. Besides, being called Mr. Edwards makes me feel I'm a character on the Little House show," he said, laughing. "We were with James for almost as long as you've been on this earth. He and I were boyhood friends, but lost touch for a time. We found each other again a few months after he lost Sara. He hired me primarily as a bookkeeper. At least that's what I was called at first. James hated tedious details, and, with his businesses growing, he found himself spending his time doing many things he didn't enjoy. He hired me to basically do all the chores he didn't want to do. It was a good arrangement because I enjoy details, and James and I never rubbed each other the wrong way. Besides being coworkers, we quickly became best friends. I guess you could say, we were as close to being brothers as two people who don't have the same mother can be."

A big yellow cat strolled into the room and under the table where it stopped and brushed its head against Riley's ankle.

"That's Max," Carol remarked. "He runs the place or thinks he does. Max showed up where we used to live five years ago and has been with us ever since. Amos still has hope of someday finding his rightful owner."

"I think Max has found his place in life right here. He's a cutie." Riley slightly leaned back in her chair to get a good look at the animal purring at her feet.

"I'll get rid of him if he's bothering you," Carol offered.

"Please don't. I love cats, and I think Max has taken to me. So, you folks have lived here in the church for just a few months?"

"That's right," Amos responded. "James bought the property as an investment. Being here on the main drag barely out of town and near Interstate 75 makes it an extremely valuable piece of property. James thought at first he would tear down the church. He said he changed his mind because it could be years before the property sold, and he could be collecting rent money in the meantime by turning it into three apartments and renting them out. But when you consider what he spent making the transformation, that doesn't make much sense. It would take a lot of years and a bundle of rent money to recover his investment. I think the truth is he had no stomach for destroying such a beautiful historical landmark. This is the site of one of the first churches built in the Adairsville area. It was once used by three different groups that rotated Sundays, each getting their turn to worship once every three Sundays. The original building burned at least a hundred and ten years ago. The one we are in now is the replacement."

"So, you think Uncle James got attached to the building before he could tear it down?"

"No doubt in my mind," Amos shot back. "Once he started the restoration, it was over. I kept warning him he was putting too much money into the project, but that didn't deter him a bit. It was his pet project and he wasn't going to cut any corners. He did it up right. A good example is that study downstairs in his quarters that he carved out of the platform area. Did you take a close look at that stained-glass window? The original window was removed before we bought the property. That gorgeous one in the center of the back wall is a replacement costing thousands of dollars. Of course, that's where he kept his book collection. I think he felt that the home for his collection had to be worthy of the honor."

"So, what caused Uncle James and you folks to decide to take up residence here?"

"I suspect James had it in his mind from the beginning that he would live here even though he said nothing about it until we were about three quarters through the job. He obviously saw how excited Carol was when it started taking shape. How could he not?" Amos smiled at his wife. "One evening when he was taking dinner with us at our house, out of the blue he suggested, 'Why don't we all move into that church building? It sure would make it handy.' We agreed, and within three months, we were all settled right here. I once mentioned to James that the day would probably come when either Carol or I or both would no longer be able to climb the stairs to our apartment. He just said, 'We'll take care of that when it happens.' I didn't know what he had in mind, but I trusted he would do what he said he would do."

Suddenly there was music. Neither Amos nor Carol recognized the tune, but Carol knew it was from a classical piece. Riley pulled her phone from the pocket of her jeans and looked at the instrument as it continued its concert. "That's Kirby calling," she announced. "I'd better take it, if you will excuse me for a minute." Riley walked into the living room, phone at her ear.

"You're right, Carol. Riley seems to be a lovely girl in every respect. It'll be nice having her with us for a few weeks."

"If I understood correctly what she implied yesterday, we'll see a lot of her even after she starts law school. I think she intends to keep her apartment here as a place to get away from the dorm. I guess it's going to be her official address."

"I don't have a problem with that," Amos replied. "That means they're planning to keep our little church home. I figured it would be one of the first pieces of their inheritance to go."

"Keeping it doesn't necessarily mean they want us around," Carol reminded her husband. "They may have other plans for our space."

"That's true, but they will need someone to take care of the place."

"And you think you're the man who can do it? When was the last time you completed a plumbing project without creating worse leaks than those with which you started?"

"I can't deny that you're right," Amos replied, scratching his head with a grin on his face. "But I do have numbers for all the plumbers in town."

Riley returned to the room with her phone still in her hand. "Kirby has been delayed in St. Petersburg. He's not likely to get away until after lunch time. That will put him here in the middle of the night. He wants to know, since everyone is likely to be asleep, if there're any instructions for his arrival."

"We plan to put him downstairs in your uncle's place. Tell him to come to the front door and ring the doorbell. I'll wait for him there," Amos told her.

"You don't have to do that, Amos. I can let him in. I'll not sleep until he's here. There's no reason for both of us to stay awake."

"I don't sleep much anyway," Amos declared. "Might as well be doing something more useful than laying on my back in the bed with my eyes wide open."

Riley gave that information to her brother before closing the call by expressing her affection. "I love you, Kirby," she declared.

"Tell me a little about your brother," Amos requested. "Your uncle always talked a lot more about you than he did about Kirby."

"That may be because I was the only girl in the family. Also, I guess I've always been a whole lot more outgoing and affectionate than Kirby. I want you to understand that doesn't mean Kirby doesn't love people passionately. He may even have a capacity to love deeper than most people. It's just that he has the kind of personality that makes it difficult to express that love. Dad often said he was exactly like his namesake, Eddie Kirby. Dad, you might know, was in the army before he went to seminary. His two best friends while in the service were Tom Riley for whom I'm named and Eddie Kirby. Dad said that like me, Tom was outgoing and more transparent than anyone else he knew while it was hard to get Eddie to say a word or ever express an emotion. Dad said we were named appropriately."

"How much older is your brother?" Amos asked.

"Almost seven years," Riley answered. "Mom and Dad tried to have children long before I came along, but it wasn't to be. There were two miscarriages between the two of us. A lot of people have told me they figured my brother and I were not close since there were so many years between us, but that's not true. I always knew Kirby adored his little sister and a major chore for him was protecting me. He was a special big brother, and I was as proud as a peacock of everything he seemed to accomplish so easily. He was the best athlete in his high school, but it was baseball he loved. After high school, he signed with the Kansas City Royals and spent some time in their farm system. First, he played in the Appalachian League with the Burlington rookie team and then one season with the Lexington Kentucky class A team. He married his high school sweetheart way too young toward the end of that first baseball season."

Max strolled back into the room and jumped into Riley's lap. She rubbed his head and she could tell by his purring that she had a friend for life. "Before being released by the Royals organization at the end of his second season, he learned that his wife was leaving him for another guy," she continued the account of her brother's life. "That guy was his best friend in high school. His heart was broken, and he hasn't been the same since. He decided to go to college. He liked Kentucky while playing baseball there, so he chose to go to the University of Louisville to major in law enforcement. Then there was the plane crash that killed Mom and Dad, and I don't think he's made much progress in recovering from that. It tore my heart and life apart, but I've managed to go on with purpose. I don't know if Kirby has. Oh, he graduated and took a job with the St. Pete Police department. He was promoted to detective a few months ago. He seems to be doing well with his job, but he just hasn't been the Kirby I used to know. I don't think he's allowed himself to get close to anyone since Mom and Dad died."

CHAPTER 2

When they heard the car pull into the drive, Riley and Amos were sitting in the front room of the downstairs apartment. Riley was reading. Amos, who "couldn't sleep nights," dozed. A glance at her phone told Riley it was just past two o'clock. She was through the door and on the front yard grass before Kirby could get out of the car. By the time he got to his feet, his sister had her arms around his neck giving him a tight hug that would do a mama bear proud. "It's so good to see you, sweet brother," she said while continuing to hold him tightly. "I've missed you so much."

"And I you," Kirby responded holding her an arm's length away from him to take a close look. "I believe you grow more beautiful every day."

A few steps from the front door, they met Amos, who had lagged to give brother and sister their moment. "Kirby, I'm sure you remember Amos Edwards from the funeral. He was Uncle James's friend and right-hand man. Amos, this is my brother, Kirby, no doubt a bit frazzled from the long drive today, but nevertheless as handsome as ever."

"Yes, I remember Amos. We also have talked on the phone several times recently." Kirby extended his hand to the older gentleman. "It's good to see you, sir," he greeted as they moved into the apartment.

Amos, as he had been the day of the funeral, was struck with the contrast in the appearances of the two. One would never guess they were brother and sister. Riley was tall and dark with medium-length hair that could probably be described as jet black. Her brother, on the other hand, had a head of hair almost blond with bright eyes that, nevertheless, looked a little sad. He was of average height, probably less than an inch taller than his sister, but slender with broad shoulders that gave evidence of the athlete he had been. Remembering their parents, Amos concluded the son resembled the mother, while the daughter looked more like her father.

"Isn't that the old church cemetery over on that hillside?" Kirby pointed to the west as he sat down.

"Yes. It's one of the oldest in the area."

"I thought it rather strange, when I pulled in here, to see a light up there at this time of the night."

Riley hadn't mentioned to anyone the light she saw the previous night, nor did she speak of it now.

"You never know what you might see in an old boneyard like that. We've heard some pretty wild tales about the spooks that wander around up there." Amos chuckled. "If there's nothing else I can do for you two, I'm going to make my way upstairs to my bed. I hope both of you'll sleep in as late as you want in the morning. You need to make up some of the sack time you missed tonight. But I would like to have a half-hour to speak with you sometime tomorrow if that works. There are two or three pending situations you need to know about immediately."

"We'll be happy to give you whatever time you need. You're the man who knows what's going on here. We're almost completely in the dark," Kirby told him.

Kirby and Riley visited for almost an hour before going to their respective bedrooms. They had talked relatively often by telephone over the past couple of months, but it was different when there was opportunity to catch-up face to face.

While in bed, Kirby realized he was lying in a spot where generations of people had sat on Sunday mornings, singing lively church tunes. Maybe some of them shouted "*amen*" when the parson's presentation got a little lively. He remembered when he, himself, was among the faithful. It wasn't that he was now an atheist. At least he didn't think so. With him, it was a matter of disappointment—a feeling of being let down. Maybe that would change in time. Maybe, one day, he wound find answers to his perplexing questions. Where was that Supreme Being when all the bad things were happening in his life? He heard his dad say, many times, that He was a loving, all-powerful, and trustworthy Father. Even though it came to him from one of the people he loved most, he was now having a hard time accepting it as truth. No, he didn't think he was an atheist. He considered himself a good person, a moral person. A code of conduct such as that espoused by the faith community, the one he heard his dad preach, was a good thing for a community. But he certainly couldn't see such wonderful love working in his life or even in the world. *If He does exist, He isn't the One to whom I was introduced in those years that now seem so long ago. But I'll let the theologians work that out. I'm just a jock turned policeman. What do I know?* With such thoughts on his mind, Kirby didn't sleep soundly in the few hours before dawn.

****

It was past nine o'clock when Kirby got up. He found the pot on the coffee maker full and a covered plate of assorted pastries beside the microwave. A cup of coffee and a warm bear claw were just what he needed before he showered and got ready for the day. About ten thirty he walked upstairs to knock on Riley's door. He didn't worry about his sister not being up. He knew she would, by now, have been stirring about for at least a couple of hours, even though the night had been short.

"Thanks for making the coffee and laying out the pastry, sis," Kirby told Riley when she answered her door.

"It wasn't me. Must've been Amos or Carol," she suggested.

"What do you think about those two?" Kirby questioned his sister. "Regardless of what direction we take with what Uncle James left us, we'll need someone here, at least for a while, to take care of our interests. Do you think we can trust them to do that?"

"I'm sure we can. They're sweet people, and I've no doubt about their integrity. I don't think Uncle James would've held them in such high esteem for all those years if they weren't trustworthy."

"Then we are in agreement that we should ask them to stay on to oversee day-by-day matters?"

"You'll get no argument from me," Riley responded. "I've only known them for a couple of days, but I think they're the kind of people to whom one could trust his life. I like them a lot."

"Then it's settled. If they're willing, we'll ask them to manage the estate. It surely will take a load off me if they'll agree."

"Of course, with Uncle James gone and them probably beyond retirement age, they may decide the time has come to step down and enjoy life," Riley offered.

"We'll give them a choice. If they decide not to stay on with us, perhaps they can recommend a replacement," Kirby suggested.

"Before we go over to Amos and Carol's, tell me about that light you saw in the cemetery last night."

"Oh, it wasn't anything to be concerned about. I just thought it strange for someone to be prowling around over there at that time of the night. You know how cops are. We're always look-ing for things that are out of sorts. It looked like two flashlights slowly moving toward the trees behind the graveyard."

"The reason I asked is that I saw a light there just about the same time the previous night. I thought it was probably some kids, but when I heard you say you saw the same thing at the same time on a different night, I wondered."

"I'm sure it's no big deal, but we'll check it out. I remember how much you liked to play Nancy Drew when you were a little girl."

"No, you've got your story all mixed up. It was Trixie Belden," Riley told him. "Always solved the case."

They found both Amos and Carol in the sitting room of their apartment. "Would you like to have a cup of coffee?" Carol inquired.

"Not for me. I just had two cups of that great coffee someone had waiting for me when I got up this morning. Incidentally, thanks to whoever did that. It was a treat for me to get up with coffee and breakfast waiting."

"Carol prepared the tray, and I fixed the coffee and made the delivery. We knew there was nothing for you to eat in the kitchen down there," Amos told him.

"Well, I suppose we need to talk a little business," Kirby said.

"Maybe I could go with you and Riley downstairs to your uncle's study," Amos suggested. "All the files are there, should we need them."

"We can do that," Kirby responded as Max walked into the room to where Riley was sitting and immediately jumped into her lap. "But before we do, there's something we would like to talk with both of you about. Riley and I have decided we would like the two of you to stay on and manage the estate. We don't know how much of Uncle James's holdings we will want to hang on to, but we expect it could take us several years to sort all that out. In the meantime, we'll need someone who knows what they are doing to take charge of things. We would want you to continue to live right here. We can negotiate the financial end of the arrangement, but we would not want you to have an income less than what you had with Uncle James."

When Riley saw both husband and wife grinning from ear to ear, she knew what their answer would be. "You can take a few days to think and talk about it if you wish," Riley offered. "But we're keeping our fingers crossed that the answer will be yes. We'll need you if we are to make the most of what Uncle James has so generously handed us. Without your help, there's a good chance we'll fall flat on our faces."

"We know what we want to do, but perhaps we need to take a day or two to give you a definite answer. We have learned it's always good to make sure that what we have in mind is what God wants for us," Amos suggested. Carol nodded in agreement.

"We would expect no less," Riley told them. "Talk about it, and then give us an answer later."

They entered the downstairs apartment without Carol. She excused herself to remain upstairs to tend to her own chores. When they came to a locked door, Amos pulled out some keys, giving one to both Kirby and Riley. "The only other key to this door is the one I have, and I will hand it over to you if you wish."

"You had better hold on to it," Kirby instructed. Riley had seen the office or study, as Amos called it, the previous day. This was Kirby's first time and his mouth dropped when the door was opened. There was a huge antique desk featuring a leather top sitting near the center of the room. But it was what was on the back wall that dominated the room: a large stained-glass window projecting an image of The Good Shepherd walking with a lamb in his left hand, a staff in his right, and several sheep at his feet. The colors in the window were breathtaking. Most of the remaining wall space was covered with beautiful bookshelves from floor to ceiling, almost completely full of books.

"This was your uncle's favorite place. He once told me he had traveled much of the world, but it was in this room, while alone, that he experienced his most complete joy. It was, of course, the platform area when still a functioning church. You saw that the lights were shining brightly from behind the stained-glass window when we came into the room. James wanted them to always be on, night and day, whether anyone was here or not. It was my job to watch the bulbs. There are three behind the glass. If one burned out, I was to replace all three to prevent any possibility of darkness."

There was a minute or two of silence as Kirby stood in awe, taking in the beautiful sight before him. Perhaps in those moments he learned far more about his Uncle James than he had learned in all the previous years of his life.

Finally, it was Riley who spoke up. "I didn't know Uncle James was such a book hound. There must be two or three thousand books on these shelves."

"He read some, but he was a relentless book collector. He would get on a plane or drive across the country to find a desired book or to get one of his books signed," Amos told them.

"But these don't look like collectable books. They look new," Riley observed.

"I think most of them were published no earlier than the 1960s and maybe the majority in the last two or three decades, but I think you will find they are extremely collectable and valuable. I don't know much about such things, but there's a man who runs a bookshop here in town, one you can trust, who can tell you about them. His name is Davis Morgan, and I would suggest you get him out here sometime today," Amos said.

"Why today?" Kirby inquired.

"One of the reasons I needed to talk with you today is that I received a call from an out of town bookseller or collector who knew your Uncle James and was aware of his collection. He will be passing through tomorrow. He wants to stop and look at the books to possibly make an offer. It might be beneficial to have some knowledge of what you have. I can give Davis a call and make an appointment if you would like."

"That would be great; don't you think, Riley?"

"Yes," Riley replied. "I don't know that we'll want to sell the collection, but even if we don't, we need to know the value of what's here."

Amos's phone rang. "If you'll excuse me for a moment, I'd better take this." Amos walked through the door just outside the study.

"Dad would have loved this," Riley said, turning her head to take in her surroundings. "It's easy to see why Uncle James loved it."

Kirby nodded and turned his face away from the stained glass. "Have you noticed the finish on those bookshelves? I don't know much about carpentry, but it's obvious that's quality work. Everything in here is first class," he added.

"That was the police chief," Amos told them when he returned to the room. "He would like for you to stop by to talk with him about James's death. He said that unless something out of the ordinary comes up, he'll probably be in his office if you would like to do so today."

"Other things can wait. I'll do that when we are through here. In the meantime, if you could line up the book guy for later to-day, we can mark that off our list as well," Kirby suggested.

"There're a couple of other things we need to talk about now," Amos told them. "Everything else can wait."

"I assume you have some idea about what you have inherited. Being the only immediate family, you are the recipients of al-most everything your uncle had, and it's significant. He left Carol and me a good lump sum of money, probably enough to see us through for the rest of our lives. On top of that, he willed us two of his rental houses that should give us another fifteen hundred dollars or so income each month. Through the years, he paid a lot of money into our pension fund. So, James has more than taken care of us. His only other bequests were some benevolent endowments and a significant gift to our church that will enable us to eventually relocate to a more visible location. You two are now the owners of eight hardware franchises scattered across North Georgia, two lumber businesses, twelve rental houses, an apartment complex with twenty-seven units, four commercial buildings that are being leased, this building we are now in and its contents, and a filing cabinet full of stocks and other invest-ments with fluctuating value, but always with a combined value in excess of several million dollars. There's also more than four thousand acres of undeveloped land scattered about that is now yours."

"Wow!" Riley responded. "That should take care of my law school expenses."

"Yes. and still leave a little pocket change for me." Kirby, who had earlier been advised of the general quantity of their inheritance, replied with a laugh.

"I don't like to dwell on the dark side of life but having worked with your uncle for all those years, I know a little about what you can expect when you receive your inheritance. There are many people in this world who want wealth but have no aspirations to work for it. That leads me to the other situation I need to tell you about. There's a young man by the name Freddy Seals who came to me recently claiming to be James's son."

"Uncle James and Aunt Sara had no children," Riley quickly reacted.

"This boy claims he is the son of James and a lady that he supposedly saw often after Sara's death. I have done some digging. I found no evidence of such a relationship. When I told him today there are scientific ways to determine the truth in such matters, he backed off. But before leaving, he suggested I write him a check for a hundred thousand dollars, and we wouldn't have to go through all that. He would let the matter drop, and we would never hear from him again. I told him you'd have to make that decision. I don't believe a word of it, but you may or may not be confronted by him."

"I'd be happy to talk with him if he shows up again. Being an investigator has its advantages in sorting through such matters," Kirby declared.

The three spent the next half-hour discussing matters such as the attorney they would need to see to probate the will. "Riley, you are welcome to go with me to talk with the police chief if you'd like," Kirby told his sister.

"No, you go ahead. I need to make some calls, and I thought I'd take my daily four-mile walk and run. I'm trying my best to hang on to that routine."

"I also want to look around town and maybe get a handle on how to find my way around," Kirby announced.

"That shouldn't take long," Amos told him with the chuckle of which Kirby was starting to grow fond. "I'll see if I can get Morgan here sometime after three to take a look at those books."

CHAPTER 3

Kirby was taken aback when he saw the small size of police headquarters. Then he remembered this wasn't St Pete but Adairsville, a town with a population of five thousand. "I'd like to see the chief, if he's available. My name is Kirby Gordan," he told the uniformed officer behind the reception desk. In less than three minutes he was walking into the chief's office. *This kid couldn't be the chief,* Kirby told himself when the young man looked up to smile at him. *He's got to be five years younger than me.*

"I'm Charley Nelson," the figure announced and reached across the desk to shake his hand. "I've been looking forward to meeting you. They tell me you're a detective on the force in St. Petersburg."

"That's right, though I've only been in plain clothes now for four months. Before that, I did my share of locking up drunks and ticketing speeders. How long have you been chief?" Kirby asked.

Charley leaned back in his chair and laughed. "You, like most people I meet, are wondering if we hire our chiefs right out of high school. I've only been chief for about as long as you've been a detective. The youngest one in the state I'm told. It's not easy, but it's working out fairly well. The jury is still out, but we've managed to keep the bad guys from taking over the town."

"Well, congratulations. It's good to see one of the younger guys in our profession getting bumped to the top. Usually, it seems to take years for one to work through the maze of time-honored prerequisites to get there."

"I guess that's one advantage of working with a smaller department. We have our protocol as well, but maybe we're not as tied to it. I wanted to see you because I felt we needed to report to Mr. Gordan's family where we are in our investigation into his death. I understand you and your sister are his only family."

"I've been led to believe Uncle James's death was an accident. Is there any reason to think otherwise?" Kirby asked, surprised by the chief's implication.

"It may have been simply a mishap. For reasons I'm sure you can figure out, we felt it best, at least for the time being, to let people think we've concluded it was definitely an accident. However, there are some concerns," Charley explained.

"And what are those?"

"We wonder what Mr. Gordan was doing out at one o'clock in the morning. According to those who knew him, that was totally out of character for him. Amos told us that for the past five years James was usually in bed no later than ten o'clock and up by six. We've found no explanation as to why he would be on Boyd Mountain, especially at that time."

"Those are certainly valid concerns, but I've got a feeling there must be more than that for you to keep this case open," Kirby offered.

"You're right. The glaring concern we have is the major wound to Mr. Gordan's head, probably the one that killed him. We don't see any way it could've been inflicted by the crash."

"So, you're saying you think he was killed by a blow to the head, then placed in his car and pushed down the hill? Have you found a motive that might've caused someone to do that?"

"No, sir. Not yet. That's another reason I thought it important to enlighten you. The one thing that stands out about James Gordan is his monetary worth. As you know, you and your sister stand to profit most from his death. If I or one of my officers have questions for you, you'll understand. I know you'll resent it, and I don't blame you. But, being in law enforcement, I suspect, ultimately, you'll understand that it's proper procedure that must be pursued. I'll tell you this: I've checked the backgrounds of you and your sister. Personally, I've no concerns whatsoever.

You may not instantly remember where you were on the night your uncle died, but I know exactly where both you and your sister were."

"But you're also mindful that we could've hired someone to do the job?"

"Logically we can't rule that out," Charley responded. "I don't believe it, but I dare not eliminate it as a possibility."

Kirby's head was spinning when he left the chief's office. *I'm a suspect in a possible murder. I can't believe Riley and I are suspected of killing our own uncle. Who does that Doogie Howser lookalike think he is?*

****

Riley usually tried to even out her walk/run routine, two miles walking and two miles running. Today she guessed she had run a good deal more than she walked. As she was finishing up the route Amos suggested she take, she decided to slightly detour to walk through the cemetery. She noticed it was not as well kept as most burial grounds. She presumed that was because the church to which it once belonged no longer functioned as the church. It occurred to her that her pastor father would've latched onto that thought for a sermon. When the church no longer functions as the church, a lot of things go undone.

When Riley saw an object to her right, she stepped in that direction and stooped to pick up a dark blue baseball cap with the Boston Red Sox *B* on the front. *One might expect to find an Atlanta Braves hat here, but it seems unlikely Red Sox attire would be common in this part of the country. I can't remember when exactly, but I know I've seen another hat like this one since I've been here.* Riley put the cap on top of one of the larger tombstones and continued on her way home.

It surprised her to realize that she already thought of her little apartment in the former church as her home. She needed a home, and she felt like she had found one. The family residence was sold after her mom and dad were killed in the accident. The money from that sale along with a small life insurance policy enabled her to go to school. For four years she mostly lived in dorms. Even two of her summers were spent on campus. She spent the previous summer with the family of a college friend in Rhode Island. Amos and Carol were starting to seem like more than dorm parents or employees. And Kirby being there just capped it off. Who would have thought the little North Georgia foothill town of Adairsville, Georgia would give her the first warm cozy feeling of home she had experienced in four years? It felt like life was starting to come together for her. She knew Uncle James deserved much of the credit. She wished she had found a way to have known him better. She thought of Kirby and wished she knew what was going on in his complicated mind.

It was almost two o'clock when Kirby returned. Riley had showered and was comfortably seated in her apartment with a mystery novel when she heard his car. She put her book down and hurried downstairs to intercept him. "Amos set up a four o'clock appointment with the book guy. That gives us time to run to one of the fast food places for some lunch unless you've eaten."

"No, I haven't, and I'm starting to get a little hungry." Kirby got back into his car. Riley opened the door to get in on the passenger side. "Where do you want to go?" Kirby asked.

"Why don't we go to Wendy's? It's nearby, and I can get a half portion of that salad I enjoy."

"So be it, Princess." Kirby guided the car toward the highway and turned east to drive above the interstate.

"You haven't called me that since I was a child. I'd almost forgotten. I fussed at you for referring to me that way, and never told you I secretly liked it."

"I think it started because, every time I saw you, you had on that tiara and long pink dress with all the ruffles. Then when you started ruling the house, I figured the nickname was appropriate."

"I did not! I never ruled the house."

"Well, maybe not, but all of us did bow to most of your wishes. Those big eyes and the way you could crawl up in a lap and snuggle enabled you to get just about anything you wanted. You never had to demand your way—you smiled and it was done. You were a spoiled little con artist."

"No, I wasn't." Riley raised her voice as she objected.

"Don't get *riled*, no pun intended. I'm just teasing. You were an adorable little girl, and I think you're still adorable. I bet you can still do a pretty good job of getting your way." Kirby laughed, glancing toward his sister before making a left turn and steering the car toward the restaurant.

Riley turned her head to glance toward the curb to her right. "That's it!" she suddenly exclaimed. "That's where I saw the Boston Red Sox baseball cap."

"What are you talking about, Riley?"

"The day I arrived, I stopped here for a salad before I located our place. When I pulled in, there was a man. I guess you would call him a panhandler, probably about your age, tall, maybe six-five standing over there on the curb with a sign soliciting aid. He wore a Red Sox baseball cap, but his hair was long enough for me to see that it was red. I noticed him because I wondered why someone here in Georgia, forty-five miles from where the Braves play, would be wearing a Red Sox cap."

"Okay," Kirby responded. "Why is that important?"

"I found a cap in the cemetery this morning exactly like the one he was wearing."

"It may very well be the same cap. Maybe the man you saw took a walk in the graveyard and left his hat there."

"I was wondering if maybe it had something to do with the lights we saw in the cemetery," Riley uttered.

"It might, *Trixie,* but I don't see why that's important."

"I don't know that it's important, but, as you might remember, I have an enormous curiosity. I like to know *why*."

"Oh yeah, I remember that five-year-old following me around the yard asking, 'Why?'"

****

It was almost four o'clock when Kirby and Riley returned to their new residence. They stepped into Kirby's flat and went straight to the study where Kirby used his recently attained key to open the door. Riley sat in one of the chairs in front of the desk. Kirby sat behind the desk with his back to the stained-glass window.

"This is such a beautiful room! I hope you won't think I'm invading your space if I come down here sometimes to just sit. It's a great place to reflect and dream," Riley added.

"You wouldn't be invading my space. This office is as much yours as mine. We're equal partners in everything here. It happens to be at the end of the living space that was assigned to me."

Glancing at the books surrounding them, Riley echoed Kirby's earlier observation. "I don't understand how these books that appear to have been published so recently could be worth any real money."

"The expert, whom Amos assures us we can trust, should be here any minute. We'll soon know what we've got," Kirby reminded his sister.

Less than five minutes passed before they heard footsteps and voices outside. Both Kirby and Riley hurriedly walked to the door when the doorbell played its musical tune. Kirby opened the door to see Amos with a couple standing behind him. "Riley and Kirby, I want you to meet two of my best friends in the world. They are Davis and Deidre Morgan." Amos stepped aside to allow the Morgans to move forward.

Kirby observed the man was on crutches and the pretty lady, who looked closer to his age than her husband's, appeared ready to give birth. Kirby held his hand out to the book specialist. "We're so glad you could help us out. You folks come on in, and we'll make our way back to the study where the books are located."

Walking the distance to the study, Kirby, at first conscious of one of their number being handicapped, walked slowly until he realized there was no reason to slow down for him. The bookman had no problem handling the crutches.

Riley walked beside Deidre. "When is your baby due?" she asked the mother-to-be.

"Any time now," Deidre answered with a smile. "I feel like I could give birth before I leave here today. The due date the doctor gave us is week after next."

"Do you have any other children?" Riley inquired.

"This will be our first together. My husband was a widower when we married. He had a daughter with his first wife. She is now grown with a child of her own. We couldn't be more excited about the baby," she declared.

"Do you know if it's a girl or boy?"

"We elected not to know," Deidre told her. "But I've noticed the doctor slipping up a couple of times to call the baby *him*. But then, I wonder if that's a smoke screen."

"Your dad was one of my heroes, Kirby. We went to the same church he had gone to as a youth. Growing up there, I heard glowing accounts of him. Before I went to college and seminary, he was already a pastor and I wanted to be just like him," Davis explained.

"He was my hero too," Kirby assured them just before they walked into the study.

"Wow." The man on crutches looked around wide eyed. "This is wonderful. I had a couple of nice studies during my ministries, but never anything like this."

"So, you were a pastor?" Kirby asked.

"He not only was a pastor, he was one of the best," Amos interjected.

"So, why aren't you still in church work?" Kirby questioned.

"I sometimes ask myself that, but it's a long dull story you don't want to hear now."

Sensing his guest wanted to change the subject, Kirby went on, "If, indeed, you decide these books are worth it, we'll have you appraise the library later, but now we just need to know generally what we have. A man will come tomorrow to possibly make us an offer. We need to have some sense of value."

The other four people watched as Davis pulled books off the shelf and opened them for a quick look. Sometimes he laid a book on the desk. And once he even appeared to sniff the inside and edge of a book before putting it back into place. All the observers remained quiet, not wanting to disturb the professional at work.

From time to time when the bookman looked at a book, he would stand up straight with an amazed look on his face. Otherwise the spectators in the room had a hard time reading him. Finally, he spoke. "This is the finest collection of modern literature I've ever seen."

"Does that mean the books are valuable?" Riley asked.

"I would say that is an understatement," Davis informed her.

"Let me show you why I say that. As a rule, the value in modern literature is in signed first editions of an author's first book, especially if that author becomes well known. When a publishing house publishes a first-time author, they don't know if his work will take off, so their run is usually small, maybe five thousand copies, perhaps smaller. If the author catches on, the numbers increase drastically with future books, sometimes climbing to the tens of thousands. Those books never become valuable because they are plentiful. It's the first edition of the first book that is valuable because it's scarce. Then, of course, the author's signature in the book adds greatly to the value of such a book. This library is full of signed first editions of first books by many of the best-known authors since the 1960s. And a key to their value is that the books and dust jackets are in almost perfect condition."

Davis turned to the books he had placed on the desk. "Let me show you a couple of examples of what I'm talking about." He picked up a book with a reddish dust jacket. "This is a signed first edition of John Grisham's first book, *A Time To Kill*. It was published by a little-known company named Wynwood. The author, at that time, had no pedigree, so they published only five thousand copies. I've heard stories about Grisham driving around, selling them out of the trunk of his car. There are many Wynwood book club editions of this book floating around and there is a Doubleday first edition that was published after a couple of Grisham's other books became best sellers, but it's this rare, signed, true first edition that is probably worth twenty-five hundred dollars or more."

Davis carefully laid *A Time To Kill* back on the desk and picked up a small book with a white dust jacket. "This is a signed first edition copy of *A Is For Alibi*, the first in Sue Grafton's private eye alphabet series. I haven't checked the value of that book recently, but I would think it is over two thousand dollars, but there's more. Before her death, Grafton got through twenty-five letters of the alphabet. Twenty-four of them, all signed, and all first editions are here. 'Y' had not yet been added to the collection, but being a recent release should be readily available, but likely not signed. My guess is the value of the set together is over fifteen thousand dollars. Some of the books on the shelves are worth only twenty-five to one hundred dollars. I suspect those are the ones your uncle had to buy at the signing events to which he traveled, in order to get that author's valuable ones signed. I won't know what the actual value of this collection is until we do an appraisal, but my educated guess is the books on these shelves have a value of well over two hundred thousand dollars. Maybe a good deal more."

CHAPTER 4

Riley and Kirby joined Amos and Carol for dinner featuring some of the best roast beef Kirby remembered putting in his mouth. It was almost nine o'clock when they finished eating, but the conversation kept them at the table for a while longer.

"I think the three of you need to know that the police chief is investigating Uncle James's death as a homicide. He believes someone hit him on the head, killing him, and then put him in the car to push him down that mountain," Kirby informed his dinner companions. "What's more, he hasn't ruled out Riley and me as suspects. He thinks one or both of us could've hired someone to murder Uncle James for his money."

"I wondered about it being an accident," Amos responded. "It wasn't like James to be out at that time of the night, and I knew him to be one of the most cautious drivers around, even at his age."

"Tell me about Charley Nelson, the police chief," Kirby requested, looking toward Amos while using his right hand to play with the saltshaker. "What kind of man is he?"

"Well, as you no doubt observed when you talked with him, he's young, and he's new to the chief's job, but I have a lot of confidence in him. He's thorough and fair. A good man. Like the Morgans, who were here earlier, he and his wife go to our church."

"Then you don't think he'll try to railroad us?" Kirby asked.

"Oh no. You don't have to worry about that. I can assure you that won't happen. You would know more about such matters than me, but isn't it standard procedure for the authorities to first investigate those who stand to gain most from that death? Isn't that what you would do if you were in Charley's shoes?"

"Yeah, I guess I would. Especially if it's a family member. Statistics demonstrate the wisdom of first looking at family. You're right. Nelson is just doing his job, but I can't help but be a little offended by someone accusing me of murder."

"Amos, do you have any ideas about why anyone would want to see Uncle James dead?" Riley asked just before Max jumped into her lap.

"I can't imagine. There was no man in these parts more generous and kinder. He respected people's rights and they respected him. Of course, he was a wealthy man and most people around here knew that. But only those of us around this table had anything to gain financially from his death."

"That may not be entirely true. It isn't always millions that lead to murder," Kirby reminded them. "Sometimes it's far less. I doubt we'll find anything, but we might do well to take a close look at the charities in Uncle James's will. Tomorrow a man is coming who is interested in obtaining a valuable book collection. I investigated a murder in St. Pete a few weeks ago that was committed for far less than two hundred thousand dollars. And Amos, didn't you say a young man claiming to be Uncle James's illegitimate son recently approached you demanding one hundred thousand dollars?"

Amos nodded. "Yes, and I don't want to judge anyone, but I wouldn't rule out anything where Freddy Seals is concerned."

"There's another factor worth mentioning. James was a curious and sometimes inquisitive man. Business and personal interests led him to do a lot of research. He was always fascinated by local history. I know it's a longshot, but maybe he uncovered something that someone wanted to keep secret," Carol suggested.

"Yeah, you might have something there," Amos replied. "It wasn't unusual for him to casually mention some intriguing fact about local history that had been completely unknown to me."

"Are you aware of anything he might have been researching recently?" Riley inquired while stroking Max's head.

Both Amos and Carol shook their heads indicating they didn't. "I do have an idea about who can help us with that. There's a young lady in town who often assisted James with his research. He knew I didn't have a lot of time to give to anything but the basics, so sometimes when he got on one of his tangents, he would secure the services of Connie Reece. She's a wizard with the computer," Amos added.

****

Riley returned to her apartment after helping Carol clean up after dinner. She turned on her TV but found nothing she wanted to watch, so she switched it off and picked up the book she had been reading. A half-hour later her phone interrupted her deep involvement in the story. She looked at the information on the screen. *Oh, good, it's Aaron,* her mind responded. "Hello Aaron, I thought you would have forgotten me by now."

"No, I still have a hazy recollection of a beautiful princess who thought she had to spend all her time in the library. How are you making out down there in the deep south? Have you started saying 'y'all' and eating grits yet?"

"I haven't heard a soul use 'y'all' since I've been here, and no one has served me grits." Riley hated to hear people stereotype southern people. Though, up to this point, she had not lived in the south; her family roots were deep in the heart of Dixie. Such statements made her feel people she loved were being painted in an unfavorable light as country bumkins. "I'm finding the people to be no less than wonderful," she told her friend.

"You would," Aaron responded. "You're the girl who could find something to like about even the worst of characters. I'll always remember you as the girl who went out with Mulely Ross."

"His name is Harold. Harold and I had a great time on both our dates. I found him interesting and very much a gentleman, unlike some other people with whom I've gone out." Riley and Aaron had dated a few times, but despite his aspirations to cultivate their relationship, Riley found she had no romantic interest in the arrogant but handsome classmate. However, for almost three years, they spent a lot of time together as part of a group of six, two males and four females. He was simply a friend whose faults she chose to overlook. They talked for more than a half hour, giving Riley an opportunity to catch up on what was going on with her friends back in Boston.

After talking with Aaron, Riley began to think about her love life. *What love life?* her mind recoiled, *I don't have a love life, but I guess that's okay. When the right man comes along, that'll take care of itself. Right now, there's law school to occupy my time.* Riley was comfortable with her current situation, but she worried about her brother. Kirby had shown little interest in pursuing any romantic relationship since his break with Sherrie. She had been the love of his life since early high school. It seemed to be all but impossible for him to get over her betrayal. Riley knew that occasionally he enjoyed the company of some young lady but was quick to back away from any serious relationships. The thought that her brother might spend the rest of his life alone greatly distressed her. She wanted to help, but what could she do?

Riley noticed it was well past midnight. *I think I'll stay awake long enough to see if our light appears in the cemetery tonight at the two o'clock hour.* After thinking about it for a while, she decided she would take it one step further. She would station herself somewhere on the hill and try to get an up-close look at who or what was crossing the burial ground at such an odd time.

At 1:30 a.m., Riley left her apartment with a dark flashlight in hand. She would use it if necessary. But if she was to stay unnoticed, she would need to refrain from using light and keep noise to a minimum. She quickly crossed the little road that ran between the church and the burying place. She made her way up the hill to the edge of the cemetery where she had a good view of most of the graveyard. She dropped to her knees behind a cluster of bushes that would help hide her but still allow her to see anyone or anything that would pass.

Riley remained in that position, listening to the crickets or tree frogs and an occasional car that passed on the main road in front of the small cemetery. Her mind began to take her on all sorts of journeys, like to the gathering of a coven of witches offering blood sacrifice. She thought of guys in white hoods burning crosses such as she had seen in books and on TV. Then there were always ghosts to consider when your immediate surroundings consisted of a cemetery. She began to think, *maybe this wasn't such a good idea. But I'm here—might as well see it through.* The young woman, who had always considered herself brave, sunk a little lower behind the bushes she had chosen as cover. She turned her head, first to the right and then to the left to assure herself she was alone. And then it happened! From directly behind her, she heard a quiet voice, almost a whisper. Her whole body went limp and her heart skipped a couple of beats.

"Trixie Belden would have brought along a partner," the familiar voice declared.

Riley's ability to move returned to her after a few seconds; she bounced to her feet and turned to see her brother standing no more than five feet behind her. "You scared the living daylights out of me. Are you trying to give me a heart attack?" she cried out before she twice pounded Kirby on his chest with her clinched right fist.

"Be quiet, sis. If anyone's around, you're going to scare them away," the obviously amused Kirby warned in a low volume voice.

"How can I be quiet when you intentionally frightened me beyond recovery?"

"Oh, you'll recover. Sit and calm down. It's almost two o'clock. If the spooks are coming on time, they'll soon be here."

Riley gave her older brother a look she wished he could see, but knew the darkness probably prevented that from happening. "What did you do, follow me up here? You didn't need to do that. I could've handled it alone," she fibbed to her brother, secretly glad he was there.

"No, I didn't follow you up here. I was already here when you arrived. I don't sleep much these days and thought I might as well check it out."

"Well, you should've told me you were coming, and we could have teamed up. That way, my heart might still be in reasonable condition."

"You just as well could've told me you were planning this little excursion and I would have been happy to join you. I think we are going to have to communicate a little better."

"Maybe so, but the truth is, I didn't plan this. It was probably after midnight before I made the decision to come up here."

"In spite of how it came together, we're here. Let's sit down, stay quiet for a few minutes, and see what happens."

Probably not more than ten minutes passed before they saw a light in the distance, obviously a flashlight in someone's hand, moving away from the fast food establishments on the north side of the highway coming toward them. "Here comes our ghost," Kirby whispered.

When the light got closer, the two investigators hiding in the bushes could see there were two men. They couldn't clearly see the faces of either man but could make out that the one with the flashlight leading the way was extremely tall. The one walking behind him was shorter than average for a man, assuming it was a man. The two people, each carrying something that looked like a bag, passed within fifty feet of them before entering the woods without saying a word.

"Let's go over to where they went into the woods," Kirby suggested after the two men had been out of sight for two or three minutes. When they got to the exact spot where the men disappeared, they saw a trail leading into the woods. Riley started to enter the woods by way of the trail, but Kirby reached out to take her arm. "Let's stop here," he suggested.

"But we still don't know what this is all about. Shouldn't we stay on their trail?" Riley insisted.

"No, we don't know that they have done anything wrong, and it's really none of our business."

"Actually, it is our business. According to Amos, we own all that property for more than a mile deep in those woods. Whoever they are, they are trespassing," Riley complained.

"Man, do we own the whole town?" Kirby asked. "Suddenly going from nothing to so much is throwing me for a loop. I'm not sure I can handle it. We'll check it out when there's daylight, but I think I know what's going on here." Kirby turned and started walking in the direction of home. Riley followed him. "I think those guys, and maybe other homeless people are living somewhere back in those woods. We keep seeing their light around two o'clock because they are going after closing time to look for food in those restaurant dumpsters and probably the ones behind the Food Lion up the road as well."

"Are you telling me those people are eating food out of a dumpster?" Riley, now horrified, asked her brother.

"Makes one feel really good about being a millionaire, doesn't it?" Kirby sarcastically responded. "I saw it down in Florida. We found around twenty people, including seven children, if I remember the number correctly, living in worn out tents in woods behind a Walmart. They were barely surviving off food they were getting out of the dumpsters."

"Kirby, if that's what's happening here, we've got to help them."

"We'll check it out. The good news is, if the situation does indeed warrant help, we're able to give it. When his sister grabbed him and gave him a tight hug that lasted for a couple of minutes,

Kirby, no doubt, suspected he would soon be a little less wealthy than he was now.

"I love you, dear brother," Riley said as she released him.

"And I love you, little sister," he responded. "Even though you're a manipulative little scamp."

CHAPTER 5

"**I** thought we would go to Cracker Barrel," Riley complained to her brother when he turned west toward town rather than toward her favorite breakfast place. "Not today. We're going to soak up a little local color. Since we seem to own half the town, we need to learn a little about it. We're going to have breakfast at the Little Rock Café in historic downtown Adairsville."

After driving the mile to the Little Rock, they were forced by a jam-packed parking lot to go around the corner to park in a spot near the police department building. "They must serve good food. There seems to be no shortage of customers," Riley noted.

"I don't know if it's the food, or if breakfast at the Little Rock is a social occasion. We'll find out," Kirby concluded just before they entered the dining room bustling with activity.

Kirby noticed five men at a table in a corner who seemed to be enjoying themselves. One of the men's eyes turned toward them, then Kirby saw his mouth move, obviously saying something to the others. Immediately all five sets of eyes turned in their direction, or more specifically toward Riley. Kirby turned his neck to face the table, glaring at the gawking men, and immediately all eyes dropped to the plates in front of them. Kirby laughed to himself, *some of the town's most prominent citizens, I suspect.*

Much to Kirby's displeasure, they were seated near the table in the corner. He didn't like being near the rowdy group of men, and probably would have requested another table, but all others were occupied. A perky woman dressed in the uniform of the day appeared at their table. "My name's Brenda, and I'll be your server." Not able to ignore the noise coming from the corner table, the waitress said, "Don't let those guys bother you. They're harmless; some of the best people in town getting together with friends for a good time."

"I understand. They won't bother us," Kirby told the waitress, feeling a little guilty for not being entirely truthful. Brenda took Riley's order and then Kirby's. It was shortly after the waitress left their table that the bookman, Davis Morgan, came into the restaurant. Seeing Kirby and Riley, he smiled in their direction before hurriedly maneuvering his crutches to come to their table.

"Glad to see you've discovered the best breakfast place in town. You haven't really experienced Adairsville until you've visited the Little Rock," Davis told them. "Deidre allows me out to have breakfast with a group of friends once or twice a week. It helps me keep up with what's going on around town, and besides, I enjoy being with the guys even though they sometimes make my life miserable. Let me know if you'd like to join us some morning, Kirby. I'll drop by your place and we can come together. I would invite you too, Riley, but I'm not sure you would be comfortable with that bunch." Davis glanced toward the corner.

"No, I doubt she would, but I'm going to take you up on your offer sometime soon. It would be good for me get to know some of the local people." *Even the raucous and unruly,* Kirby thought. "I hope you didn't forget your phone," Kirby told Davis. "According to what Deidre told us, a quick trip to the hospital might be required at any time."

"It's right here," Davis patted his pocket. We live about three minutes away. I left her in bed. She only grunted and turned her nose up when I offered to prepare her breakfast."

"I know she's excited and ready for the baby to make his or her appearance," Riley spoke up.

"We both are," Davis declared. "I'd better get over to our table, or the guys will be through before I get started. I'm glad I ran into you. You two have a great day."

"He's a nice man," Riley told her brother.

"He seems to be. Time will tell," Kirby replied.

"I guess this is what you call a country breakfast," Riley suggested when Brenda delivered plates overflowing with food. "I don't think I've ever seen so much food on one plate."

Kirby took a bite of bacon. "Now we know why there were no vacant parking spaces."

After a few minutes one of the gentlemen from the corner table, the best dressed of the group, got up and came toward them. "I'm Al Jensen," the man in the dark suit and red tie told them. "I don't want to interrupt your breakfast, but I thought maybe I needed to come over and introduce myself."

"Good to meet you, Mr. Jensen. I would shake your hand, but I probably have a little bacon grease on my hands," Kirby told him, looking at his fingers. If the remark made Jensen feel guilty for disturbing their breakfast, then it had served its purpose.

"I'm the manager of the Adairsville Bank. The one Mr. Gordan used. He had several accounts with us and as a matter of fact, was on our board for several years. We're hoping you will continue to do business with us."

"We'll see, Mr. Jensen. I'm still learning the ropes, still dependent on Amos Edwards in such matters. At least for the time being, we'll leave things pretty much the way Uncle James had them set up."

"Please know that I'm available to help in any way I can. You can usually find me in my office at the bank most Mondays through Fridays. Incidentally we're the largest bank in town," the banker added before walking back toward the corner.

"Well, you might know it was the banker that came over to meet us. Amos told me that Uncle James had accounts with all three of the banks in town. He thought it important to support all the legitimate businesses possible," Kirby related to his sister. "Better get to work on that food. We've got a busy day ahead of us."

When they got up from the table, Kirby reached for his wallet to leave the tip. He noticed that Riley left half her food on the plate, a reminder to Kirby of why Riley seemed to have no trouble remaining slim and trim while he had to spend so much time in the gym. Kirby's plate was empty. "Hope you folks enjoyed your breakfast and will come back to see us soon," Brenda told them. Kirby paid the check and they headed for the door.

****

"Do we have time to check out what's happening behind the cemetery before we meet the man who wants to buy the book collection?" Riley asked just before they arrived back home.

"I think we do. It would be good for us to include Amos in our trip to the woods if he's available. I told him what I suspect this morning before we left. If there are people living back there, he can help us decide what steps to take next."

Amos consented to go along. They were soon on their way across the cemetery to the edge of the woods where they discovered the trail the previous night. The three walked briskly, mostly in silence, with Kirby leading the way, Riley behind him, and Amos bringing up the rear. After about ten minutes they saw three tents pitched under a large oak tree. There was a fire pit in front of the campsite, obviously for cooking. To the surprise of all three searchers, they saw three children playing near the tents being supervised by a lady who looked to be African-American.

"Good morning!" Kirby shouted, approaching the campsite.

Almost immediately, five additional people came out of the tents, three men and two women. The tall redheaded man who Kirby guessed to be about thirty-five years of age, stepped forward and shyly asked, "Can we help you?"

"Yes, you can," Kirby answered. "I'm Kirby. This is my sister Riley, and our associate Amos. We think we own this property and we need to be clear about what you're doing here."

"You *think* you own this property?" the tall man questioned with a puzzled expression.

"It's a long story," Amos replied, "but I can assure you the ground on which you are camped belongs to Kirby and Riley."

"Okay, then let me promise you we're doing nothing wrong here. We just need a place to stay," the tall man answered.

"We understand. We're not here to make trouble for you. Perhaps we can help you," Riley spoke up.

"Would you introduce yourselves to us?" Kirby requested.

"Sure," the tall man said reluctantly. "I'm Bill, and this is my wife, Judy," pointing toward a brunette who looked to be about a foot shorter than her husband. "The boy and girl you see standing over there are Eddie and Faye, our two children, three and four years old. These folks are Jessie and Alice." He motioned toward an African-American couple. "And this is Juan and Louise, and their daughter Lois." The third child, a little dark headed beauty looked to be four or five years old.

Kirby suspected all the names came from Bill's imagination, but it didn't matter to him. His experience told him it would be pointless to try to get a lot of information about why they were here and in such a destitute situation. Riley walked over to where the children were and knelt on the ground to try to converse with them, but obviously their timidity stifled any real conversation on their part, even though their smiles directed toward the beautiful lady spoke volumes. Kirby and Amos continued to try to pry information from the adults, but it was clear Bill was the spokesman for the group and wouldn't be forthcoming with any pertinent information.

"You're free to stay here for now, but we're going to have to work out something better for down the road," Kirby offered after a few minutes of trying to feel his way. "I don't want you scrounging food late at night like you've been doing. Later today, we'll get enough food and water out here to last you three or four days. If you will promise me to keep your noses clean, I'll work on something more permanent for you, but you must behave yourselves. Do you understand?"

"We get it," Bill replied. "We would appreciate anything you can do for us."

"If you'll stick with that, I think I can help you get on your feet, but you're going to have to want it."

Strolling back down the trail, the trio made plans to get groceries later in the day and recruit a friend to use his Jeep to get the provisions to the campsite. Amos would set the plan in motion.

When they returned home, they found Carol with Rayford Barnes who had arrived early to examine the book collection in which he was interested. "Where are you from?" Kirby asked Mr. Barnes.

"I live in Birmingham, Alabama, but grew up in Atlanta," the middle-aged man answered.

"How did you know Uncle James?" Kirby further inquired.

"I knew him from our mutual interest in books. I believe we first met at a Pat Conroy signing in Atlanta. After that we visited at several such events in a couple of different cities. We had dinner together a time or two. He often spoke of the collection he was building. When I heard he was killed in an accident, I thought I would check to see if his books might be on the market. Are you a book lover, Kirby?" Rayford asked.

"I read a lot, but I know next to nothing about collecting. What about you, Rayford? Are you a collector or dealer?"

"Like a lot of book people, I'm both. I have a small bookstore just outside of Birmingham in the Center Point area, but I have hundreds of books I would be hard pressed to give up."

Riley accompanied the two men to the study to view the books where, as always, they found the light behind the stained-glass window shining bright. "Here they are," Kirby told him pointing to the shelves. "Look to your heart's content."

He knows his stuff, Kirby decided as Rayford coolly examined the books without showing any emotion. *He doesn't want us to expect there is anything worth any real money on the shelves.* Their visitor took about a half hour to study the collection. Kirby sat behind the desk with the stained-glass window to his back. Riley was seated across the room where she could enjoy the beautiful window. Finally, the bookman pulled out a pad on which Kirby assumed he was tabulating.

"These books are in new condition and many of them are author-signed, but they are recently published books. I haven't found an older collectable among them. Some of them may have some real value in fifty or seventy-five years from now, but, of course, I'm not going to be around then to reap the benefits. But maybe I can help you out. I'll take them off your hands if you'll accept five thousand dollars for the bunch."

"Five thousand," Kirby muttered. "Is that your top offer?"

"Maybe I could come up with another thousand," Rayford offered after standing, silently looking at the ceiling for a few moments. "But that's the best I can do."

"Okay. We're going to have to pass, Mr. Barnes. We can't let them go for that."

"I'll tell you what I'll do, I'll give you fifteen thousand *dollars*," Barnes said, "if you will let me pay half now and half in three months."

"That would work out well for you, wouldn't it, Mr. Barnes? You could sell ten or twelve of the better books that are in great demand over the next three months, completely recouping your money and what you owe us, and still have hundreds of great books to keep you in the black for some time."

"Where did you get the idea those books are worth that kind of money? I made my offer in good faith. You can take it or leave it."

"We know for a fact that the collection is worth in excess of two hundred thousand dollars because there are so many signed first editions of first books by celebrated authors. I think we'll refuse your offer, Mr. Barnes."

"There may be some valuable volumes there, but a dealer can't pay full value for a book and make any money when he turns it over."

"I understand that, but a fair offer even from a seller for these books should exceed eighty thousand dollars. That still leaves a profit margin of well over one hundred thousand dollars."

Rayford Barnes turned to walk out of the study. "Incidentally, Mr. Barnes, when and from whom did you hear of Uncle James's death?" Kirby asked.

"I don't know why it matters, but I was in Atlanta the day after he had the accident and heard it on the TV news."

"Maybe you could leave me a card so we could get in touch with you should we decide to negotiate further," Kirby suggested.

Barnes handed him a card and stomped out of the room muttering something about people who know nothing about books.

Before they left the study, Kirby suggested to Riley that they discuss the squatters on their property above the cemetery. "I've been thinking about it, Riley, and it occurs to me that we may have an opportunity to do something good for those three families. Have they put themselves in the position they're in? Maybe. Are they deserving? I don't know. But what I do know is Mom and Dad taught us that you don't evaluate the reason for the need, you see the need and try to do something about it. Maybe we can do that on a larger scale than we've been able to do before."

Riley's face lit up like a Christmas tree. "Tell me what you have in mind."

"Amos informed me that we have five empty apartments in our complex of twenty-seven. Why can't we keep three of them for benevolent purposes, rent free or whatever the people can afford? We could put our three families on the hill in those apartments rent free for the next two or three months and after that, maybe for half rent or less. We could, with Amos's help, find a supervisor for starting and overseeing a commercial cleaning company which we could use to provide jobs for Bill, Jessie, and

Juan. We'll find used furniture for their apartments and provide food until they get their first paychecks. You understand this is going to cost us some money. There will be equipment to purchase, a work van will have to be secured. In the beginning, it may be only our own businesses that will be interested in the services of our cleaning crew. I suspect it would take a couple of years to start seeing any real profits, and our friends may not work out at all. They may not want to work," he added.

"It's a wonderful idea," Riley responded. "I wish I'd thought of it." She had been proud of her brother when he signed to play pro-baseball. She was super proud of him when he decided, on his own, to go to college and then graduated high in his class. But she had never been prouder of him than she was now, and she told him so. She just wished he could somehow successfully handle his personal demons.

Neither Kirby or Riley, after eating such a big breakfast, were able to eat the sandwiches and chips offered by Carol for lunch, but they did take the opportunity to sit around the table and sip her special iced tea while bouncing off their ideas about the apartments and the cleaning crew. Amos and Carol were thrilled. Amos immediately thought of a qualified man who he believed would be overjoyed to have the opportunity to lead that business. Amos and Riley would discuss the idea with the three men when they used Davis's Jeep to deliver the food later in the day. They agreed the new business would be called TCC for The Cleaning Crew.

CHAPTER 6

A young lady who appeared to be about five years younger than Kirby appeared at the door shortly after he rang the doorbell. *Carol wasn't joking; she is rather attractive,* Kirby determined after only a quick glance in her direction.

"You must be Kirby Gordan," she said with a welcoming smile.

"Yes. Guilty as charged," Kirby responded, thinking, *that was a dumb thing to say.* "And you are Connie Reece."

"Come on in and find a seat. Mom is out back watering her flowers but will probably finish in a few minutes. I appreciate you calling before coming. Mom and I like having company, but we don't much like being caught off guard."

"Just a matter of courtesy," Kirby responded.

"So, you're Mr. Gordan's nephew. I remember him telling me you once played professional baseball. Which team were you with?"

"I was with the Kansas City organization, but I lasted only a couple of seasons. That was a while back. They discovered I couldn't hit a good curve ball. That cut my baseball career short. I'm now with the St. Petersburg, Florida police department. Are you a baseball fan?"

"I love it. Mom and I attend four or five Braves games a year and go to Rome, maybe five or six times a season, to see the Rome Braves play. We can be found in front of TV watching a game most evenings during the season."

"I'm glad to hear that. I don't know too many girls who are deep into baseball. But, I'm not here to discuss your sports preferences. I understand you did some work for Uncle James. There're a couple of questions I have about that. I was told you're a computer whiz, and Uncle James sometimes sought your help to gather information."

"I wouldn't call myself a computer whiz, but I do enjoy that kind of work. I was finishing my college degree by driving each weekday to Dalton State. Your uncle found out I needed to supplement my income. I think he first assigned me projects because he knew I needed the money. Evidently, he liked my work and continued to bring jobs my way. He paid me well, which was a blessing for me and Mom. I had only known him in passing before, but he and my dad were friends for years before Dad died."

"Tell me about those assignments. What kind of research did he have you do?"

"It varied. Sometimes it was to check up on the health of a business, or maybe he needed information about some potential investment. From time to time he wanted to know more about some local or semi-local event from the past. It seemed to me he had a keen interest in local history, especially of the little-known variety. I always thought a lot of those searches were more to satisfy his own curiosity than to gather information that would aid him with business ventures. For example, in our research we once came across an unsolved murder of a government agent who was sent to town back in the late-1930s to investigate illegal moonshine traffic. The reality that the case had never been solved, after all these years had passed, bothered him to no end. We worked on that for weeks before we were able to identify the obviously guilty party, of course, long since deceased. But knowing the case had been solved, at least to his satisfaction, seemed to appease him. He didn't like loose ends."

"I didn't know that about Uncle James, but it makes sense. My dad, Uncle James's brother, was like that. He would never let go of anything, no matter how small or insignificant, until it was neatly tied up. Both my sister, Riley, and I have uncommon curiosities that cause us to push without letting up until we find suitable answers. I guess that's one reason I was recently promoted to detective. Tell me about what you were working on with Uncle James in the days before his death."

"In the three or four months before his accident, I worked on three projects. One was typical. He was interested in a lumber business in Chatsworth. The company was over fifty years old and changed ownership three times in those five decades. Like always, he wanted all the details he could get. I assumed he was interested in purchasing the company. It was pretty much routine. The current owner, a Mr. Anderson I believe, had owned two previous businesses with neither one doing very well. This one seemed to be going down for the third time." Connie paused and glanced to her left when she heard a subtle noise made by someone walking into the room. "Mom, this is Mr. Gordan, Mr. James's nephew. This lady is Beth Reece, my relentless mother who is determined to have the best-looking flowers in Adairsville or at least in the Maple Village development."

Kirby stood and took several steps toward the lady who was removing her large floppy hat. "Call me Kirby," he instructed. "I figure I need a few more years before I deserve to be addressed as 'mister.'"

"Then Kirby it is," she responded with a smile. "As for the flowers, the weather doesn't seem to be cooperating. Don't think they're going to win any awards this year."

Kirby knew immediately he would like this lady who reminded him of his own mother. "I've been quizzing your daughter about her research for my uncle. I hope you don't mind. I have two or three more questions. Then I'll try to get out of your hair."

"We'd be happy for you to stay a while. I bet Connie didn't offer you any iced tea. I'm going to have some. Could I bring you a glass?"

"I think I would enjoy that," Kirby replied.

"And what about you, Connie? Can I bring you some tea?"

"No Mom. I think I'll pass."

After Mrs. Reece left the room, Kirby again turned to her daughter. "Connie, you mentioned the research on the lumber business you were doing for Uncle James, but you stated earlier there were two other projects in those months before his death. May I ask about those?"

"Both of them came out of some prior research I did for him. A few months back, your uncle apparently met a man by the name of Earl Lance. I think he was applying for a job at one of your uncle's businesses, maybe as a manager of one of the hardware stores. To make a long story short, we could find no trace of him until 1981 when he was twenty years of age. Mr. Gordan asked me to look at newspaper accounts, and other sources, to see if I could find anything prior to 1981 that might explain a person suddenly appearing in 1981 after not existing the previous twenty years."

"And what did you find?" Kirby asked.

"Not much. I found an account of a nineteen-year-old convict who escaped from authorities this side of Dalton in 1980. He was being transported from Atlanta back to Chattanooga. We found no record of him ever being rearrested after his escape. If I remember correctly, he was a hit-and-run driver of a car that killed an elderly lady. It would be a long shot, but maybe there was no record of Lance's early life because he was that convict and successfully came up with a new identity after escaping. More likely, he found another life far from here. The other incident we investigated was a 1961 fire out in a rural area near Tate where the house burned with several members of the family escaping. However, an infant in the house was never seen again. The strange thing is they never found any trace of him in the ashes. It was thought to be a case of arson enabling someone to kidnap the baby. However, no one ever contacted the parents with any ransom demands for his return. The timing would be about right if that missing baby turned out to be Lance. I doubt if either of those cases have anything to do with Mr. Lance, but that's all we found."

"Does Earl Lance live around here?"

"I think he resides near Rome. I feel sure Mr. Gordan never hired him, but you probably can find the folder of material on him in your uncle's files. I put together reports on the escaped prisoner and the house burning that should also be there."

Mrs. Reece came back into the room. She handed Kirby a glass of tea with a napkin beneath it. "I hope you like it," she said. "We Georgians enjoy our sweet tea."

Kirby knew why when he took a sip. It was delicious.

"I'm going to need to go," Kirby told the ladies. I have an appointment in Cartersville with Uncle James's attorney. I guess he wants me to sign some documents related to the will." After finishing the drink in his hand, Kirby got up to start toward the door. "I'm the executor of Uncle James's estate. After a few weeks, I will likely not be around often, and my sister will be in law school at Emory. Amos Edwards will be overseeing our business interests. I wondered if you would be available if we needed you from time to time to do the same kind of work you did for Uncle James?" he inquired.

"Yes, I would be open to that as things stand now, but I'm looking for a permanent business position. I don't know where that might take me in the future."

"I hope to see you soon," Kirby said as he walked through the door.

****

Kirby was visiting with the girl who helped Uncle James with research. He would then go to Cartersville. Amos was out tying up loose ends to get TCC off the ground. Carol invited Riley to go with her to a meeting of her quilting bee, but Riley declined. Now she found herself at home alone, wishing she had gone with either Kirby or Carol. After a few minutes of quiet solitude with a book, she heard a car pull into the drive. Shortly afterward, she was aware someone was walking around outside. She laid her book down and left her apartment to go outside by way of the stairs at the side. She walked around the corner and called out, "Can I help you?"

A young man, perhaps close to her own age, came around the other corner of the building. His clothes were baggy and looked as if he had slept in them. He badly needed a haircut. When his eyes focused on Riley, a mischievous grin came to his face. "Who're you? I haven't seen you around here before."

"I'm Riley Gordan and I live here." She shifted her weight from one foot to the other, trying not to show her uneasiness in the presence of the unfamiliar visitor. Riley had always argued that everyone deserved a chance beyond first impressions. Seeing the way this stranger now leered at her was making it hard for her to practice what she preached. "Can I help you?" she again asked the young man with the wicked grin.

"You can help me," the intruder laughed. "Yes, you can. You're a looker. A beautiful girl like you could help me a lot."

"Who are you?" Riley asked as she took one step backward.

"Don't be scared," the man with the roguish manner told her. "I think we're cousins. Maybe we could be kissing cousins. My name is Freddy Seals and the old man who lived here was my father. I'm here to get what's coming to me."

"You'll have to talk with my brother about that. He should be back any minute," Riley added.

"I don't see him," Seals declared after turning to look behind him. "I guess you and I will just have to talk about it. If you don't want to talk, I have some other things in mind we could do."

"I suggest you get out of here as quickly as possible. You could find yourself in some serious trouble. My brother is a policeman, you know."

"I see that both old Amos and his wife's cars are gone. I guess that means we're all alone." Freddy Seals snickered as he took two steps toward her. She took one backward.

It was then that Riley heard the voice from beside the building to her right. Seals could not, at first, see who was speaking, but he could hear the words. "Do you need us, Miss Riley?" the course voice asked.

Riley started breathing again when she turned and saw six-foot-five Bill walking in her direction with the shorter Juan to his right and the muscular Jessie on the left.

"Who're those guys?" Seals asked, taking a step backward while keeping his eyes posted on the newly arrived trio, now a few feet away from Riley's side.

"They're my friends," Riley declared with a big smile on her face. "Bill, Jessie, and Juan are The Cleaning Crew. Guys, this is Freddy Seals, and he was about to leave. Weren't you, Mr. Seals?"

"Uh, I guess I was," he responded while turning to go back to his vehicle. Just before getting into the banged-up, old Chevrolet pickup, he turned and said, "I'm going, but I'll be back."

"Please do, Mr. Seals, but be sure to call before you come and make an appointment with my brother. I'm sure he would like to talk with you."

The wheels of the pickup squealed as the driver stomped on the accelerator to make his exit. "Where did you guys come from?" Riley asked in a tone that revealed her relief. She turned toward her three protectors. "I was never so glad to see anyone in my life. You were there precisely when I needed you."

"You were there precisely when we needed you," Jessie, whose voice she had not yet heard, responded.

"Mr. Amos left us up at the campsite to pack some of our belongings. He was to return for us, but we got through quickly and thought we would walk down here to let him know we were through," Bill told her. "We heard what was going on and thought you could use our help."

"You got that right. I'm not sure what would have happened had you not come along. You gentlemen have my eternal gratitude," Riley assured them. "Amos will probably be by in a little while looking for you fellows. Would you like to wait in my apartment? I think I have enough soft drinks for everyone, and maybe I can even come up with some sandwiches."

"We appreciate it Miss Riley, but we had better stay here where Amos can spot us when he returns," Bill responded.

"Please do me a favor and just call me Riley. The "miss" in front of my name makes me a little uncomfortable."

"We can do that," Bill told her.

"Since we are going to wait out here, why don't we sit down over here on the little retaining wall?" Riley suggested.

They all found a seat. "These guys don't talk much, but I want you to know that we all are grateful for what you and Kirby are doing for us. None of us have had a place to live for a long time. Our wives and children are especially glad to be able to live like real families. People have sometimes given us a couple of dollars or even occasionally as much as a twenty, but no one has ever done for us what you and Mr. Kirby are doing. We'll never forget it, and we'll be here for you anytime you need us. We're not going to let you down," Bill assured her. "I've made some mistakes in the past, but I have another chance to get it right, and I'm not going to blow it."

"We're able to help you because of a loving uncle who was extremely generous with us. It wouldn't be right for us to hoard everything for ourselves. It's called *paying it forward*," Riley told them. "We help you and you help someone else and the world gets to be a better place quickly."

They talked for a while before Amos finally returned in the service van. The white vehicle, perhaps three years old, had already been decorated with dark green letters on both sides about nine inches high that simply said, "THE CLEANING CREW."

"We are going to have to get you guys licenses so you can drive this thing," Amos told them as they were crawling into the van.

"But I never learned to drive," Riley heard in a voice with a Spanish accent.

"We'll fix that," Amos assured Juan. "I'm a good driving teacher."

"I don't want to be aboard when he lets Juan get behind the wheel," Jessie laughed.

Riley remained outside enjoying the Georgia sun until Carol returned. "Anything interesting happen while I've been gone?" Carol inquired.

"Let me tell you about our new friends," Riley excitedly said to the older lady. "How do you feel about the existence of guardian angels?"

When Riley returned to her living room a few minutes later, she picked up her Bible to thumb through Hebrews to find a verse she thought was in that book. After about five minutes she found it: *"Do not forget to entertain strangers, for by so doing some people have entertained angels without knowing it."*

CHAPTER 7

When not on the job, Sundays were hard for Kirby. For many years it was a day of worship for him. Since that was no longer true, he never seemed to find anything to do on the first day of the week that felt right. Riley went to church with Amos and Carol. He was in his apartment with a cup of coffee. The TV was set on some political program, but he had little interest in the discussion.

Kirby's mind was swirling with possibilities about Uncle James's apparent murder. The suspects were starting to pile up, though none yet jumped out at him. Because of an obviously shady disposition, he could not eliminate the Birmingham bookman, Rayford Barnes; though it did seem illogical. He had difficulty believing one man would kill another for a collection of books. After what Riley told him about Freddy Seal's visit, he figured the punk was capable of just about anything. Then there was Mr. Anderson, the Chatsworth lumberyard owner, whom Uncle James found to be less than reliable in business. *However*, Kirby decided, *that's not grounds for murder.* The top suspect was perhaps Earl Lance. The accounts of the escaped convict, and the possible kidnapping of an infant, needed to be investigated. He decided his next step would be to find Lance. He knew he needed to search Uncle James's files to see if there was any information there that would tie Lance to either of those items. Maybe that's where the answer lies. There could be a motive here if Lance was the convict, or even if he were the kidnapped baby. Maybe Uncle James put it all together, and Lance knew he was in trouble. But his investigation had just started, and the guilty party could very well be none of those people.

Kirby was headed toward the kitchen with his empty coffee cup when his phone rang. "Kirby, this is your old pal, Monroe. Long time, no see. How are things down in Florida?"

It took Kirby only a few seconds to identify the voice on the phone even though it had been three or four years since they last talked. Monroe Thompson was a high school friend with whom he played both baseball and football. "Yes, Monroe, it's good to hear your voice. How've you been?"

"Doing well, and enjoying my non-stop crazy life," Monroe told him. "Marie and I occasionally talk about taking a little vacation down there. The kids want to go to Disney World. Maybe we'll show up on your doorstep some time."

"I'd love to see you and your family. Presently, I'm in Georgia, but will be getting back to St. Petersburg in probably two or three weeks."

"What're you doing in Georgia, of all places?"

"My dad's family originally lived in a little town in the northwest part of the state. Dad's younger brother remained here until he died a few weeks ago. Riley and I are all the family left. We're here trying to tie down some estate matters. What's up, Monroe? After all this time, you didn't call me just to talk."

"You're right. I've got some bad news. I know how much you once loved Sherrie. I thought you needed to know that last night they found her dead on her sofa. She's dead, Kirby. Sherrie is dead."

"Dead? They found Sherrie dead. How could that be?" Kirby's whole body went numb. "She's just twenty-nine years old. How could she be dead? What happened, Monroe?"

"The report is she committed suicide. She took a handful of her prescription medication. I think it was medicine she took for depression. I understand she tried the same stunt, without success, a few months back."

"I had no idea she was going through anything like that," Kirby mumbled. "We've had no contact in almost four years, and, with me several states away during that time, I received no news about her and Casey. I guess I wasn't anxious to hear about them because it just brought back the whole mess which triggered the hurt all over again."

"I understand, Kirby. The word I've gotten is that things haven't gone well in their marriage for the last two or three years. I was told Sherrie wanted children, but they were unable to have them. Then there was their drinking. Both had started to drink way too much. You know how that goes."

"Yeah, I do. From what I've seen as a policeman, I think to drink at all is to drink too much."

"Sorry to be the bearer of such bad news, but knowing the kind of guy you are, I knew you would want to know."

"I appreciate your thoughtfulness, Monroe. You're a good friend. You and the family come on down to Florida and visit me sometime soon." By now, Kirby hardly knew what he was saying. It seemed his mind had stopped working. He couldn't think. Over and over he heard the words Monroe had spoken, "Last night they found her dead on her sofa. She's dead, Kirby. Sherrie is dead."

When Sherrie left him, Kirby didn't shed tears. He remembered sitting alone in a dark room night after night asking, "Why?" *What could I have done differently? How could I have made Sherrie love me more?* And in time he began to ask, *how could she and Casey do this to me? She was my wife and he my best friend. How could they do this?* But he never cried. Now, he could not hold back the tears. They freely flowed down his cheeks. *Why am I reacting this way? I despised her. Then why am I so broken up? She destroyed my life, and I lose it when I get word she's gone.* The longer he thought about it, the clearer it became. He lost Sherrie six years ago, but he never stopped loving her. Through all the anger and resentment, his love for her persisted. All through those bitter years, deep down, he still loved her. The reason he found no other during that time wasn't that he was afraid of being hurt again. It was that he had found no one who he could love enough to replace Sherrie. He still loved her despite all that had happened between them. His love for her was so deep that it survived all that she had done to him.

****

On their way home from church, Carol announced to Amos and Riley that it might be as much as an hour before lunch would be ready, but she assured them, "It'll be worth the wait. I'm going to prepare my special southern fried chicken."

"It's like nothing you've ever eaten before," Amos told Riley. "And the great thing is, it comes with all the trimmings."

"I can hardly wait," Riley told them. "Mom used to fix fried chicken, and I remember how good it was. I think Kirby loved it even more than I. It'll be a pleasant surprise for him."

"You love your brother a whole lot, don't you?" Carol asked more as a statement than a question.

"I guess it shows," Riley told her. "He's always looked after and protected me, and I've loved every minute of the attention. I guess when I was a little kid and he was the high school jock, I placed him on a high pedestal. He's been up there ever since. And now that we just have one another, I think he's even more dear to me."

Carol turned toward Riley, who was sitting in the backseat. "If I could get to you, honey, I'd give you a big old hug and assure you that you and Kirby have more than each other. You have me and old Amos here. We know we will never be your mother and father, but we're going to love you just like you were our own kids."

"Amen," Amos called out from the driver's seat. "You two are already family."

"To hear you say that makes me happier than you could know. I do worry some about Kirby though. He's had a rough time over the past few years. He never dated any girl but Sherrie before marrying her shortly after turning twenty years of age. With him being a baseball player, he was away much of the time. Sherrie stayed home during the season when he was playing in North Carolina and then later in Kentucky. She was young, and I think immature. She was lonely. My take is that led to her starting up a relationship with Kirby's best friend. Before he finished his second season, while they were still newlyweds, she announced to him, she and Casey were in love and she was going to get a divorce and marry him. Well, Kirby fell apart. He finished the baseball season just going through the motions. I still believe he could've eventually made it to the majors if this disaster had not come into his life. But that is just an evaluation of one who knows little about baseball but a lot about the baseball player. Their marriage lasted less than a year. Still grappling with the failure of his marriage at the end of the season, he was released by the Royals. Then, on top of that, Mom and Dad were killed in that plane crash. Kirby hasn't been the same since." At this point tears began to form in Riley's eyes. "He's still a good man, but I'm afraid his heart is torn to pieces. He seems to be going through the motions, and I'm so concerned about him."

"Don't you worry, honey," Carol told her. "He's a smart man, and he's had a proper upbringing. He's goanna come around. We're going to love and encourage him."

"You're going to learn mighty quick that we're not perfect, but we'll stick with you through all the bad times, as well as the good. You can depend on us. Most importantly we are going to pray for him," Amos added.

Riley had not felt as secure since her mom and dad perished in that plane crash four years earlier.

****

Kirby heard the vehicle pull into the drive. Riley and the Edwards were home. He got up, went to the bathroom, and washed his face. Five minutes later, he heard Riley's footsteps and then the knock on his door. "Come on in Riley, and sit down."

Riley strolled toward the chair nearest her. "Carol says lunch will be ready around 1:30, and guess what? We're having fried chicken." It was then that Riley noticed her brother's eyes were swollen, and the look on his face was his serious expression, usually reserved for only extremely troubled times. The last time she saw that look was when they received news that Dad and Mom were gone.

"There's something I need to tell you, Riley. Do you remember Monroe Thompson?" he asked.

"Yes, I remember him," she reluctantly spoke. "He was the big guy, loud and friendly. He used to constantly pick at me when I was a little girl and you two were in high school."

"Yeah, that's the guy. He called about an hour ago to give me some disturbing news. He told me they found Sherrie dead on her sofa last night. Evidently it was suicide. She apparently intentionally took an overdose of her prescription medicine, and it killed her."

"Kirby, I'm so sorry. Despite everything that happened, I know you loved her." Riley got up from her chair to take a few steps to where he was standing. She embraced him tightly, laying her head on his shoulder. They both found seats on the sofa after a few moments. Riley continued to hold his hand.

"You're right, I did still love her. I don't think I realized that until this morning, but it's true. I had not lost my love for her. Even though we were not together for six years, and I had not even laid eyes on her in the last four, she was still the love of my life. She was on my mind every single day of those six years. Riley, I think my greatest regret for the rest of my life may be that I didn't forgive her until she was gone. I wonder if I'd forgiven her and then told her of my change of heart, if she would still be alive. I know it would've saved me six years of misery. I remember hearing Dad say the one who holds a grudge is hurting himself far more than he is hurting the one he resents. I know now exactly what he meant, because, I experienced it for six years."

"I'm sorry she's gone, Kirby, and I'm appalled she left this life the way she did, but my concern is for you. Maybe it seems like it came too late, but the fact is you've come to grips with your true feelings. You've forgiven her even though it's no longer possible to tell her so. The point is, you *have* forgiven her and now you can get on with your life."

"Maybe," Kirby told his sister. "I don't know. I'm sort of numb. We'll just have to see how the future plays out. I got online to check out the arrangements. The funeral is Tuesday in Watertown where she and Casey lived. I want to be there. I've already made a reservation to fly into Logan late tomorrow."

"I'll go with you. I have nothing planned. There's no reason I can't go."

"No, sis. I appreciate your willingness, and I know it's because you care about me, but I would rather make the trip alone. It'll give me time to think about things."

Riley hated the thought of Kirby on such a mission all alone, but as much as she despised the idea, she knew it was best. It always mystified her that Kirby had been most adept at working through things when he isolated himself to ponder through his problems. He needed solitude while she was just the opposite. She needed to *talk* with someone about her troubles. "I'll drive you to the airport," she told him.

"I think I'd better drive myself and park there, so I'll have my car when I return. It's not like we must count pennies anymore, Riley. We can afford the parking garage at the airport," Kirby reminded her.

****

Riley ran ahead of Kirby to the Edwards' dining room to alert them of Kirby's sad news. When he arrived both Amos and Carol expressed their sorrow over the turn of events and gave him a comforting hug. When Amos gave thanks, he made Sherrie's death and those left behind a matter of prayer. However, they each, without discussing the subject, knew they needed to give Kirby some space. If he wanted to talk about it, they would. If not, they would converse about other things. It was obvious he didn't want to talk.

"I almost forgot," Carol told them. "Yesterday at my quilting bee meeting, Edna Plank told me something interesting that you two may need to know. She has a grandson named Tony who, I think, is about twelve or thirteen years old. He and his buddy Eddie, who is a couple of years older than him, like to go camping. Their favorite place to camp is on Boyd Mountain, a short distance from where they live. Edna said when she heard the rumor that James's death might have been murder instead of an accident, she remembered something from several weeks previous. She said Tony came in early on a Saturday morning from one of those camping trips, and he wasn't himself. He sat around for the rest of the weekend without saying much, acting as if something was bothering him. She said she thinks that was the same weekend James was killed. She wonders if maybe the boys might have seen something about which they are reluctant to talk."

Immediately Kirby raised his head. "That might be the lead we need," he suggested. "When I get back from Massachusetts, we'll follow-up. Just don't mention this to anyone. If the boy saw anything, we'll encourage him to go to Chief Nelson."

Receiving such promising information seemed to improve Kirby's mood. He participated more freely in the conversation during the remainder of the meal, but the troubled look on his face remained throughout lunch and the rest of the day.

When Riley had Kirby to her apartment for a light supper, his brooding disposition was once again in evidence. It broke her heart to see him this way. When darkness came, Riley, alone in her bedroom, wept. She cried for the one who was once an important part of her life, now gone. She cried for her brother whose heart was broken, and she prayed.

CHAPTER 8

Before Kirby left for the airport, he suggested to Riley that she might want to go through Uncle James's files. He instructed her to look for anything about a Mr. Anderson from Chatsworth or Earl Lance. She was also to keep an eye out for information about an escaped convict or anything concerning a house fire that might've been a cover-up for a kidnapping. She was sitting in the desk chair behind the big desk in Uncle James's study. The rollers on the chair allowed her to move to the file cabinets and take out a section of files. Then with a push she would roll back to the desk with the folders in her lap. She made several such trips in the first half-hour without finding anything of interest. *Uncle James could have used instruction on how to set up a filing system,* she decided. A few minutes later she struck pay dirt in one of the lower cabinet drawers filed under "local interest." There Riley found folders containing information about both the convict and the house fire. She put those on the desk and continued to search.

In another fifteen minutes Riley also had information in hand on Anderson and Lance. The file on Lance looked as if it was basically information gathered for the purpose of evaluating a potential employee. There was a resume, a completed application, references, and background checks from two sources. The important thing was that they now had an address for the man missing the first twenty years of his life. She went back to pull several files from the "local interest" section that had earlier caught her attention. Evidently Connie Reece was indeed Uncle James's go-to researcher. In almost every file folder, "research by Connie Reece" was neatly written inside at the top. Riley sat at the desk for another forty-five minutes studying the information gathered. When she finally departed the study, she left all the interesting folders on the desk where Kirby could find them later. She hurried to find Carol. She had promised her they would take a walk together before dark. On her way up the stairs Riley met Max who was obviously looking for her. She knew that because he produced the friendliest of purrs when she leaned over, picked him up, and held him with his paws over her right shoulder.

****

Not wanting to talk with anyone, Kirby laid his head back against the headrest and closed his eyes to pretend he was sleeping. Even though he wasn't a veteran air traveler, flying little since the crash that killed his mom and dad, he had flown enough to know some people will not be deterred from conversation. They insist on talking despite their seat companion's wishes. Kirby clearly was assigned a seat beside such a passenger.

"You going to Boston?" the big man wearing glasses asked in a voice louder than necessary.

That's where the plane is headed, was Kirby's thought. But the words that came from his mouth were kinder, though not dripping with warmth. "Yes sir. I'm going to Boston." He hoped that would end their conversation, but that was not to be.

"I've lived in Boston for almost thirty years. You live there or just going for a visit?"

Good for you, Kirby mocked in his mind, but answered, "I used to live in the suburbs, but only visiting today."

"Going back for any particular reason or just visiting family and friends?" the boisterous stranger asked.

Can't you see I don't want to talk, mister? "I'm going back for a funeral," Kirby answered.

"Who died?" the big man asked with more volume than required, allowing everyone nearby to hear.

"Someone I loved very much. My ex-wife," Kirby muttered, turning his head and body toward the window, hoping the man would take the hint. Evidently, he did because he finally was silent.

The hardest part of this whole ordeal is going to be facing Casey. What'll I say to him? I guess I'll know when the time comes. Kirby's thoughts went back to the happy times he and Sherrie had together. Their first date was the middle school dance just before finishing the eighth grade. He could still visualize that yellow semi-formal dress she wore on that occasion. He didn't remember what he wore, but he had never forgotten any detail about her appearance. He had decided two years prior that she was pretty, but it was on that night he knew she was beautiful. It was the occasion of their first kiss. He knew it was an awkward peck of a scared middle schooler on his girlfriend's cheek, but a moment he could never forget. When people talked of his high school days, they usually spoke of his triumphs as an athlete. Athletics rated high with him, but high school was about Sherrie. Sherrie was at the center of just about everything he held dear from those years. During the midseason break, he, a young baseball player head-over-heels in love, came home for the wedding. It was the happiest day of his life. He always believed it was Sherrie's most special day as well, but maybe that wasn't true.

Rehearsing his years with Sherrie made the plane ride from Atlanta to Logan pass quickly. They were on the ground, starting to exit. "I'm sorry about your loved one. May God bless you in your bereavement," the big man who had the seat next to Kirby told him.

Kirby felt a warmness for the passenger that had escaped him previously. He was ashamed of his earlier attitude. "Thank you, sir. I appreciate your thoughtfulness. You have a nice day."

****

Though Riley was already thinking of the converted church building as her home, she still had not learned to sleep soundly there. During the nights she heard every sound that occurred in the building. She knew Kirby was in Boston, but she was awakened by what sounded like someone banging into a piece of furniture in the apartment beneath her. She listened closely for the next fifteen or twenty minutes, trying to decide if it was her imagination or if someone was moving around in Kirby's quarters. She looked at the clock on the stand beside her bed to see that it was almost a quarter after two. Amos or Carol wouldn't be down there this time of the night. A while later she heard a car start in the distance. She could hear it moving away from her until the sound was out of earshot. No other sounds came from beneath. Riley went back to sleep.

Remembering the noise, the previous night Riley decided after she had her coffee and toast to walk down to the lower apartment to see if anything had been disturbed. Everything looked intact until she came to the study door. It was slightly ajar. She was sure she was the last person to be in that room. She distinctly remembered closing and locking the door. She hurried into the room where, as always, the lights behind the stained glass were highlighting the Good Shepherd. Looking about, everything seemed in place. Then she remembered the file folders she left on the desk. She turned to see if they were where she left them. There was nothing on top of the desk. The folders were gone. *Amos has a key; perhaps he, for some reason, came down and retrieved them.* It didn't seem likely, since Amos had been out for most of the evening, but no other explanation came to mind. *Unless someone broke in and stole them. But why would anyone want those? There was no evidence of such a burglary, despite thinking she heard something being bumped last night. But, truth be known, that was almost a nightly occurrence.*

Riley ran upstairs to find Amos, but he was not in his apartment. "Is Amos around?" she inquired of Carol, who was running the vacuum cleaner.

"He's outside spraying the roses," she told Riley. "Can I help—" but Riley was gone, heading toward the stairs that would take her outside.

"Amos, you out here?" she yelled.

"I'm over here." She heard his voice coming from around the corner, and rapidly moved in that direction.

"Amos, I left some file folders on the desk in the study late yesterday. Did you move them?"

"No, honey. I haven't been in there in two or three days."

"I thought I heard someone down there in the middle of the night, but I'm always hearing things in this old building, so I sort of dismissed it. When I checked this morning, it looked as if nothing had been disturbed except the door to the study was unlocked and slightly open. The folders I laid on top of the desk for Kirby were gone."

"We'd better call the police," Amos urged.

"I left my phone lying on a table in my kitchen," she told Amos. "Can you call them?"

Amos pulled his phone from his pocket and punched the appropriate buttons. Ten minutes later, with Amos and Riley standing outside beside the entrance to the front door, two young officers drove into the drive in their dark-colored cruiser.

"I understand you folks had a break-in," the officer who had been behind the wheel said to them when he was within a few feet of them.

"So it would seem," Amos responded.

"I'm Jed and this is Mike. If you'll tell us about it, we'll see what we can do for you."

"Riley lives upstairs, directly over the downstairs apartment. She heard something down here last night but didn't pay much attention to it. She checked this morning to find the study door slightly ajar, even though she locked it when she left there late yesterday. Her search inside the room revealed some file folders she had placed on the desk were gone," Amos explained to the officers.

"Did the folders contain anything valuable?" Jed asked as the group minus one officer walked toward the study.

"Only information. I don't think they had any monetary value," Riley responded.

"Who else lives in the uh . . . house?" the officer asked.

"My brother is temporarily staying down here," Riley said. "Mrs. Edwards, Amos's wife, lives upstairs with him. Kirby, my brother, is currently in Boston for a funeral, and Carol hasn't gotten anywhere close to that room in several days," Riley answered, sounding a little irritated.

"No evidence of a forced break-in at the door or any of the windows that I can see," Mike, the younger officer announced.

"No damage to this door," Jed stated when shown the study door.

"There may be no damage to any of the locks or windows, but someone took those files. It's not my imagination. Whether you believe me or not, I did leave several file folders there on top of the desk, and they were taken some time during the night," Riley told the officers.

"I don't doubt your story. I'm just saying, evidently, whoever took them had a key, the ability, or tools to open both the outside door and the door to the study." Jed looked toward Amos. "If I were you, I'd change those locks and perhaps install something a little more difficult to get past."

"It will be done before the day ends," Amos told Jed.

"Do you have any idea why someone would want those folders?" the officer asked.

"No clue," Amos answered.

"Are you sure nothing else was taken?" Mike, the younger officer, who couldn't seem to keep his eyes off Riley, asked her.

"I'm fairly certain, but with everything that is in here, it's hard to say for sure. Some of the books are enormously valuable, but I don't see any holes where any have been taken. Amos and I will go through the room after you've gone. If we find anything else missing, we'll let you know."

"We'll keep a close eye on things for a while. Don't panic if you see headlights in your drive in the middle of the night. Our officers will make you a regular part of their patrols. Don't hesitate to call us if you see anything suspicious," Jed told them.

"It was sure nice meeting you, ma'am," Mike grinned in Riley's direction when the two officers turned to return to their car.

"I think that young officer, Mike, was sort of captivated by you, young lady," Amos stated to Riley as the officers were driving away.

"Oh, Amos, you think every young man that comes around is falling in love with me." *He was sort of cute, but maybe a little backward. I don't think he said ten words.* Riley picked up a pad lying on a nearby piece of furniture. She wrote down the address she had seen earlier in the folder for Earl Lance: 146 Mason Lane, Rome, Georgia. It was one of the times when her exceptional memory paid off.

****

Several of the old high school crowd greeted Kirby when he entered the funeral home. Not knowing exactly what to say to him, most of them said little beyond the standard remarks one would make to a friend they had not seen in a while. No one even mentioned Sherrie to him, except Jessica, who he remembered as one of her closest friends. "It's really bad about Sherrie, isn't it?" she said, holding his right hand in both of hers.

"It sure is," Kirby responded without elaboration. "How's Jon?" he asked about the man he remembered as her husband, hoping they were still together.

"He's fine, just as ornery as ever." Kirby was relieved to hear her reply.

Kirby saw Casey standing near the open coffin. This guy who had once been his partner in almost everything he did had instantly become the one person he had no reservations about hating. This man betrayed him in the worst way one man can betray another. It was a cancer that had eaten at him for more than six years. As he watched Casey greeting those who approached him, bent and broken, looking twenty years older than his twenty-nine years, the years of animosity toward the man all but left him. He didn't understand it, but he found himself feeling compassion for his one-time friend. Kirby, not wanting to make a scene, stood at a spot away from Casey and the open coffin.

Then Casey spotted him. At first, he looked surprised, but after the shock wore off, he did not hesitate to leave the row of people lined up to greet him. He almost stumbled over a family member's feet as he hurried toward his one-time best friend.

"Kirby, I'm so happy you're here today. For so long I've wanted to ask for your forgiveness. We treated you so badly. I know it probably means nothing to you now, but I don't think I can live with myself any longer without telling you that I know we inflicted a lot of pain on you, and I'm sorry. You cannot imagine how much I need your forgiveness. I know I don't deserve it, but to receive it would give me reason to go on."

"You've got it, my friend." Kirby heard himself saying words he never expected to say. "I forgive you, and I forgive Sherrie." The two of them locked in an embrace. The tears flowed as they shared both a deep sorrow and a newfound release. Kirby understood they would never be best friends again, but they both had found relief that would enable them to live their lives with a peace they had not known in recent years. The buzz in the chapel almost stopped with everyone standing quietly, gawking at the two men they thought might throw punches when they met again.

****

Kirby heard but did not follow much that the presiding pastor shared in the funeral message. It became obvious to him that the preacher probably had not known Sherrie well. He did not know for sure, but suspected Casey and Sherrie did not regularly attend any church.

Kirby thought about what forgiveness meant. He had more than once heard it said that one cannot forgive unless he completely wipes from his mind the transgression against him. The argument went that if one remembered, he had not forgiven. Kirby could not imagine that being possible. How could he completely wipe Casey and Sherrie's reprehensible actions from his mind? He didn't think he could do that, but he could eliminate those offences from his heart. The key to forgiveness, he decided, is the ability not to be negatively affected by those memories when they do occur, to love the offenders despite their transgression. Maybe forgiveness had to do more with the heart than the mind. *Maybe that's not forgiveness at all. Maybe there's more to it, but whatever this is, it's certainly helping me.*

Later when Kirby boarded the plane to go back home, he knew they had done it to him again. "You going to Atlanta?" his seatmate asked.

"That's where I'm headed," he told the inquisitive gentleman. "I assume that's your destination as well."

"No, I'm changing planes in Atlanta. My destination is Miami."

"I live in St. Petersburg," Kirby told his newfound friend, "but I'm currently, through circumstances I'll not go into, caught in a place called Adairsville, Georgia."

"Well, as long as you get back to Florida by winter, you'll be okay."

"I suppose so, but Adairsville isn't half bad. I'm starting to adjust to it. It has lots of history and loads of interesting people."

"Such as who?" the gentleman asked.

"Oh, no one whose name you'd recognize; except maybe, baseball hall of famer Bobby Cox or Vic Beasley who plays for the Falcons. Cox married a lady from there, and they have a farm outside of town. Beasley grew up there. I've never met either of them. But I'm meeting a lot of just good downhome people."

"Better watch out. It sounds to me like you could end up living there permanently."

"I don't know about that," Kirby responded; then added, "We'll see what the future brings."

CHAPTER 9

Riley and Carol left after lunch to travel to Floyd Hospital in Rome, hoping to be among the first to see Deidre and Davis Morgan's new baby boy. Amos and Kirby decided to look at the place where Uncle James's car left the road before they visited with Tony, the boy Carol told them about. Amos insisted on driving. Kirby, in the passenger seat, commented on the beautiful older houses they passed on Park Street.

"There was a time when this was called Society Hill," Amos informed him. "Most of these houses have been restored. Gives you an idea what the historic district once looked like."

Amos pointed to the left when they came to the bottom of the hill. "I don't remember it, but they tell me there was once, over there, a park from which the street got its name. I do remember the public pool being at this location when I was a boy. I used to spend a lot of my summertime hanging around there flirting with the girls and listening to the juke box."

"What did Carol think about that?" Kirby asked with a laugh.

"She couldn't care less in those days. She didn't know I was alive. She was still swooning over a guy name Rance Tobin. I don't know what happened to ole Rance. I think I'll get Connie to check that out for me."

"Carol might be able to tell you," Kirby suggested, chuckling.

"Oh, I doubt that. Once she got to know me well, she forgot all about him and every other guy she dated." Amos grinned at his companion.

"Sounds like you were a real ladies' man."

"Still am!" the older gentleman, with a twinkle in his eyes, assured him.

They came to the stop sign where they halted before crossing Halls Station Road to start up Boyd Mountain, which was little more than a good-sized hill. After driving about a half mile on the upward sloping road, Amos pointed to the left. "That's where it happened. We'll drive on up to the top and turn around, and park on that side of the road."

A minute or two later, they pulled into a long drive that led to a handsome white house. "That's what the locals call 'High Lonesome,'" Amos explained as he was turning the car around to head back in the direction from which they came. "That's the Boyd house, and thus you have Boyd Mountain. I don't know if you have noticed or not, but you can see it from just about anywhere in town. Maybe a little more so in the winter when the leaves don't block the view."

Amos pulled off the road as much as he dared. From this point Kirby could see through the trees and bushes a few of the houses and businesses in downtown Adairsville. His detective persona took over. "No curve or anything I can see that would cause one to lose control, but it would be the best place for a car, pushed off the road, to go down the hill a way before hitting a tree."

"I'm going to walk into the woods across the road," Kirby said, already marching in that direction. Amos followed him.

"Watch out for poison oak," Amos warned.

Entering the woods, Kirby looked for a flat spot. Most of the terrain was sloping. "If two boys were going to set up a tent here, they would look for a level place to pitch it." Kirby found his level spot after three or four minutes. He saw something caught in a nearby cluster of bushes. When he strolled over to pull it out, he discovered it was an empty potato chip bag. Holding it in his left hand, he walked back in the direction of the flat ground. He bent down to get a closer look; then leaned over to pick up something. He held up a cigarette butt for Amos to see. "Potato chips and a cigarette. What would you expect two middle school boys, camping by themselves, to do? They might figure it's a good time to experiment with smoking, and they surely would bring potato chips. What middle schooler can make it through a Friday night without potato chips?"

The two friends got back into the car and headed toward the bottom of the mountain. "Well, Tony may not be home, but we know he's not in school. Summer vacation has started." Kirby pointed toward a group of children playing on an empty lot shortly after turning left off Park Street. The elementary school was only a block away. Tony lived with his family across the road from the front of the school.

"How well do you know Tony?" Kirby asked.

"I'm not as well acquainted with him as is Carol, but I know him and his folks well enough that they will recognize me."

"That's true of just about everybody in town, isn't it?" Kirby asked.

"There was a time, Kirby, but our little town is growing, and I have to admit there are a good many people with whom I'm not acquainted." Amos turned into a drive that enabled them to pull up beside the porch of a small frame house. "This is it. Let's get it over with," Amos suggested, opening the car door. Kirby quickly got out and followed him to the door.

"Can I help you . . . oh, Amos. Good to see you. How have you and Carol been?" A lady at the door in jeans and a blue checkered shirt greeted them.

"We're doing just fine, Gail. This handsome young man over here is Kirby Gordan, James's nephew. We were wondering if it would be possible for us to talk with Tony about one of the camping trips he and Eddie took a couple of months back."

"I guess Mama must have told you how he was acting after returning home that weekend that Mr. James was killed."

"Well, she didn't tell me, but she did mention it to Carol. You know how those ladies talk at quilting meetings."

"If you let us speak with the boy, I promise we will try our best not to upset him," Kirby remarked.

"I'm not worried about that. I've known Amos for a long time." The mother grinned. "He's across the road, in the school yard. He's supposed to stay where I can see him, but it looks like he's nowhere in sight. You'll find him over there somewhere. Go ahead and have your talk. Maybe you can get something out of him. I can't."

The car was left in the driveway while the two men walked across the road. They saw two boys on the lower side of the complex. "That's Tony." Amos pointed to the taller of the two boys.

"That wouldn't be his camping buddy, Eddie, would it?" Kirby asked, looking at the other boy who was using his thumbs on each side of his mouth to make a funny face for the benefit of his companion.

"No, Eddie is older and a little taller than Tony. I don't think I know that boy. Hi Tony." Amos smiled at the boys as they drew near.

"Hello Mr. Edwards. Have you seen Half-Pint lately?" The boy laughed at his little joke.

"No, not lately. I figured Nellie was more your speed." Amos laughed with him. "Tony, this is Kirby Gordan from Florida. He's Mr. James Gordan's nephew and he wants to talk with you for a moment if that's okay."

"He's a policeman, isn't he?" Tony immediately asked.

"I'll see you later, Tony. I've got to go home," the other boy declared.

"Yeah, Kirby is a policeman down in Florida, but he's off duty, and I promise he won't bite. We're here as your friends."

"Okay." Tony drew out the word making it sound like a complete sentence.

"Your grandmother told Mrs. Edwards that you were camping on Boyd Mountain on the night Mr. Gordan was killed there. She thought you might have seen something that maybe would help us figure out what happened," Kirby suggested.

"If I saw something, will I get in trouble for not telling it sooner?" the boy asked.

"No, son, not if you tell us now exactly what you saw," Kirby assured him.

There was silence while the boy reflected, trying to decide where to start. "Eddie said we should just get out of there and keep everything we saw to ourselves."

"If everyone did that, we would have a hard time setting wrongs right in this world. I know you were scared, but tell us what you saw, and we'll make sure no harm comes to you," Kirby told him.

"It was the middle of the night when two cars stopped on the opposite side of the road from where we were camping. We got behind some bushes to watch. It looked like two men were moving an unconscious person from the passenger side to the driver's side of one of the cars. Knowing what I now know, I figure that had to be Mr. Gordan. When they got him behind the wheel, they pushed the car down the hill, and it crashed into a tree. When the men left, I thought we should go down there and check on the man in the car, but Eddie thought we should pack up and get out of there. So that's what we did. We agreed not to tell anybody, but maybe that was wrong."

"Tell me about the men," Kirby requested. "Did you know them?"

"No, I don't think I knew either one."

"Were they tall, short, fat, skinny, old or young? Is there anything you can tell me about them?"

"They just looked like men. I guess just normal average men. I was scared and I didn't pay much attention to how they looked."

"What about the car they drove away in? Did you notice anything about that?"

"No, not really. I think it was a dark color, and something made me think it might have been pretty new, a late model car, but that's all I know."

"Did you hear the men say anything?" Kirby asked.

"The only thing I remember is that one of them said something like, 'You don't think they will figure out the car was pushed off the road?' The other one answered saying something like 'This is Adairsville. Gibbs don't live here and there's no NCIS.' I remembered that because I watch NCIS every Tuesday night. Then I think he said, 'Our boys will never figure it out.'"

"Is that exactly what he said?" Kirby asked. "Did he say, 'our boys'?"

"I'm pretty sure he did."

"You've been very helpful, Tony. Now let me tell you what we want you to do. We'll tell your mother that you did see something that must be reported. We'll explain to her you need to go immediately to Chief Nelson, today if possible, and tell him everything you can remember. We'll alert him you're coming. He's a good man who likes boys like you. You can count on him doing everything possible to help you. Will you do that?" Kirby asked.

"Yeah," Tony answered. "I'll go today, if it's okay with Mom."

"Good man," Amos responded. "I knew we could count on you."

Kirby and Amos walked back across the street. "We still don't know who was responsible for Uncle James's death, but we do know a good deal more than we knew when we got up this morning. We know for sure it was murder. We know it was two ordinary looking men who did the deed. One of them is evidently an NCIS fan, and apparently he is a local resident," Kirby surmised.

"How do you know he's local?" Amos asked.

"Tony said he was sure one of the killers referred to the authorities as 'our boys.' That causes me to believe he is a local citizen."

"That makes sense, but I never would have come to that conclusion," Amos remarked.

When they got back to the house both men went to the door to talk with Tony's mother, but Amos did most of the talking, being the one who knew her best. She agreed that she and Tony would go without delay to see Chief Nelson.

Returning home, they stopped by the police station to inform Charley of what they had learned and to tell him that Tony would be coming for a visit. Kirby expected a reprimand from Nelson about him having no jurisdiction here. The chief offered no such rebuke. "Be careful. It looks like there are some dangerous characters roaming around out there. I know I don't have to tell you that they probably highly resent you sticking your nose into their business," Charley told them on their way out.

They found Riley and Carol already home when they arrived. "Tell us about the new baby," Amos requested.

"Beautiful baby boy with a head full of dark hair, weighing a little over eight pounds. Looks as healthy as any baby I've ever seen."

"I got to hold him," Riley bragged. It was at that precise moment, as if he heard and became jealous, that Max jumped into Riley's lap.

"I'm glad you got back. Mr. Rittman called. He and his daughter Sheila are coming over to meet Kirby and Riley at three-thirty," Carol announced.

"I was wondering when he would show. I expected he would have been around earlier," Amos said.

"Who's Mr. Rittman?" Kirby asked.

"Judson Rittman is our number-one citizen, or at least that's how he thinks of himself. His family goes back to shortly after the town came into existence. He claims they were here before the Cherokees were driven out. There was a time when the family was wealthy. They once owned a good deal of property in these parts. Judson's grandfather had some money back in the depression when no one else did. A lot of people with property but no money were glad to trade land for a little money to feed their families. That's when the old man bought up just about everything he could get his hands on. Judson's dad Layton wasn't as shrewd in business as his dad. Judson would never tell you, but by poor management, he has lost much of what remained of the family fortune. I'm not telling you this as gossip, but you need to know what's going on when you meet Judson. He hung around James as much as he could. I don't know if it was for appearance or if he expected to get something out of him. Maybe he thought James's skill and drive would rub off on him," Amos speculated. "He's a proud man. That's probably the main thing I can tell you about Judson Rittman. He's a man who will do just about anything to protect his status in this town."

"His daughter Sheila is a beautiful girl and a couple of years older than Riley. I understand she's been engaged twice, but the weddings never happened. Word from the quilting bee is that Judson is looking for someone deserving and wealthy enough for his little girl," Carol told them.

"And if it came from the bee, then it's gospel." Amos laughed.

"Don't you poke fun at those precious ladies," Carol spoke with a little indignation in her voice. "Those are my closest friends."

"I would never make light of you ladies. Why, that's the best group of ladies to be found in this town," Amos, trying to redeem himself, said. "I tell you what, though," Amos went on. "Kirby, you better be ready because little Miss Rittman will have her cap set for you."

Kirby blushed. "I guess that comes with the territory. It's not easy being a rich and handsome young tycoon," Riley suggested, adding to her brother's embarrassment.

It was almost four o'clock when the Rittman's finally arrived. So much for punctuality. It didn't take Kirby or Riley long to figure out that Amos and Carol were right on target with their assessment of both father and daughter. Sheila was an attractive girl, wearing a skirt a few inches too short. She appeared stymied by her father's presence. He tried hard to make her shine. Such an effort was unnecessary. It was obvious she needed no help in that department.

Judson had a lot of questions about their inheritance. Those were mostly directed at Kirby, but Riley was not ignored. Even if they had chosen to do so, they couldn't answer most of those questions because they still had not made many of the decisions they would have to make in the coming weeks.

"Incidentally, I need to tell you something I discovered recently. I believe there's a band of homeless people living on your property up behind the cemetery. When I figured out what was happening, I thought about calling the law to them, but I decided that was your business. If I were you, I would do something about that as soon as possible," Judson declared.

"Oh, it's already been taken care of," Kirby told him.

"So, you had them locked-up?"

"No sir. I found them places to live and gave them jobs," Kirby responded.

"You did what? You realize you aren't helping our community by encouraging people like that, don't you?"

"People like what?" Kirby asked.

"You know, people who are lazy and refuse to work. People from other ethnic groups, criminals and thieves."

"How can you know anything about the character of the people living on my property? Did you take time to get to know them?"

"No, I just know the way they are. They wouldn't be homeless if they had any real moral fiber."

"You've lived a lot longer than I, Mr. Rittman, and maybe you're wiser. I don't know. I learned as a child that it's a mistake to judge people without even bothering to check out their circumstances or getting to know them," Kirby told his guest.

Sheila was smiling when they exited the apartment, but Judson didn't look happy. *I'm afraid I didn't make a good impression,* Kirby decided as Mr. Rittman and his daughter drove away in their shiny Cadillac. "So much for that. I doubt the distinguished gentleman will want his beautiful daughter to have anything to do with me."

"Oh, he won't let a thing like that little disagreement remove the target off your back," Amos assured him. "Not as long as your bank account is up to par."

CHAPTER 10

C onnie and Beth Reece often enjoyed going to Manning
Mill Park after dinner to walk Beth's five-year-old bas-
set hound, Ralph, named for one of her childhood boy-
friends. The dog and the boyfriend had similar ears. The mother and daughter were considered by others, who frequented the
park at that time of the day, as regulars. "If we hurry, Mom, we'll
have time to walk around the track at least once before dark,"
Connie told her mother after putting the last dirty dish in the
dishwasher. Beth called for Ralph and attached the leash to his
collar while Connie pulled the car out of the garage, stopping
out front for her mom with her beloved hound to enter the car.

"I ran into Carol Edwards today at the beauty shop. She told
me that young man, Kirby Gordan, has just returned from his ex-
wife's funeral in Boston," Beth told her daughter.

"Oh, I didn't know he had an ex-wife," Connie responded.

"According to Carol, he married young, and it didn't work
out."

"Well, I guess that's what you would expect from an arrogant
rich guy. They go through wives like everyone else goes through
socks."

"You shouldn't be so judgmental, honey. He didn't strike me
that way at all. He seemed like a nice young man."

"You're right, Mom. You raised me better. I shouldn't be criti-
cal of people I don't know. It's just that I've known his type before, and that seems to be the common pattern in that crowd."

"Before you start placing the Gordan boy in any group, you
need to know all the facts. He's just now come into money. Kirby
is the son of a preacher, and I've never known any preachers who
were rolling in money. His dad and mom were killed in a plane

crash on a missionary trip a few years back. Both he and his sister managed to get their college degrees, and he's worked as a policeman for a while. That's not your typical rich boy," Beth concluded.

"I guess not, but please Mom, do me a favor. Don't start playing matchmaker again. I'm not interested in him or anyone else I know right now. Let me do my own choosing."

"Now, honey, when did I ever interfere in your life? I've never done that."

"No, not more than a dozen times. What about Jerry Payton or that red-headed guy who claimed to be on his way to Harvard but never finished high school?"

"All I did was introduce you to them."

"That and arrange dates for me," Connie responded.

"You can be sure I'll not try to help, ever again. If you end up living alone your whole life, don't blame me," Beth declared while turning her head away from her daughter. She didn't say a word for the remainder of the drive to the park.

They got out of the car and started their walk around the three quarters of a mile track. By that time, Beth had forgiven her daughter sufficiently enough to at least talk to her again. Connie loved the view this walk provided. The walking trail took them around a small lake. There was a patch of woods on the side of the lake farthest away from the parking lot. Connie had more than once warned her mother not to walk there alone. The terrain on the back side of the park provided an ideal place for any kind of scoundrel to hide and pounce on his prey. Despite such warnings, Connie learned after the fact that a couple of times her hardheaded mother had thrown caution to the wind and walked Ralph along the winding trail by herself.

Ralph became fascinated with the ducks as they rounded the lake to start on the straight stretch of path along the southside of the park. He stopped to announce his presence with loud yelps while pulling on the leash that Beth held, attempting to get to the birds.

"That dog's going to get away from you, Beth, if you're not careful." The voice was that of Kerry Evans, a widower who lived near them, now going in the opposite direction than the two ladies.

"That's the reason you are eager to come out here to walk. Your boyfriend's always here," Connie said to her mother when Mr. Evans was past hearing distance.

"You know he's not my boyfriend. Who's doing the matchmaking now?"

"Okay, I'll keep quiet, but don't blame me if you end up living alone the rest of your life," Connie responded with a smirk.

"You've made your point. Now let's move on to something else," Beth said, glaring at her daughter.

Connie heard something in the bushes to the right. She turned, barely able to see a figure behind a big rock raise his head enough to be seen. That head was covered with something like a navy ski mask. Then she saw him raise an object to the top of the rock. It took her only a moment to realize it was a rifle and it was pointed in their direction. "Look out, Mom," she cried before taking two rapid steps in the older woman's direction to pounce on top of her and take her to the ground. As they hit the ground hard, both ladies heard the shot. Connie realized as a result of the dust flying from the ground beside them that the shot barely missed.

In the fall, Beth let go of the leash and now Ralph was running loose, dragging his leash behind him swiftly moving toward the figure in the bushes behind the rock. The shooter, seeing the dog running toward him, turned to flee in the opposite direction. It only took Ralph a few seconds to catch him and latch on to his right pant leg. The shooter threw down his rifle and used both hands to pry Ralph loose from his pants. When he had accomplished that, he threw the dog as far as he could back in the direction from which he came. He picked up his rifle with his left hand and again began to run.

Ralph, obviously stunned by the blow he received when he hit the ground hard, stood and whimpered before starting to slowly move back toward his mistress. The shooter disappeared into the woods. Connie saw Kerry Evans running toward them. She got to her knees beside her mother. "Are you all right, Mom? Don't try to get up until we make sure nothings broken. Call 911. Someone shot at us," she cried out to Mr. Evans, who was now near.

Two policemen were on the scene within five minutes. In little more than ten minutes, the EMTs were there. The shooter was able to escape. The two ladies were found to be physically okay, though Beth would, undoubtedly, experience soreness for a couple of days. Ralph appeared to have escaped serious injury and was given an extra treat later that evening when he was allowed to sleep on the foot of Beth's bed. The two ladies where at a complete loss as to why someone would shoot them. It had to be mistaken identity they decided. Nevertheless, they were pleased to observe police cars regularly drove slowly past their house throughout the night. Despite her confusion about what had happened, Connie was able to sleep after an hour or so of lying awake. She knew the chief of police, Charley Nelson, well. She had even dated him a couple of times back in his single days. He would watch after them even if he had to personally do the job.

****

"Don't tell Carol I said so, but I think the coffee here is even better than what she makes," Amos declared after taking a sip from the cup the waitress delivered to him.

After a long session in Cartersville with Uncle James's long-time attorney, Amos insisted they stop by the Little Rock for a cup of coffee. The little restaurant wasn't nearly as crowded as it had been when he and Riley had breakfast there, but it was apparent that Amos knew all the patrons, as well as the on-duty staff. Kirby suspected it wasn't the coffee that drew Amos, but rather the social opportunity it provided. After they were seated for a while, Chief Nelson came through the door with a big man. Spotting them, he led his companion to their table.

"I want you to meet my big brother," he told Kirby. "Kirby Gordan, this is Dean Nelson, the best mechanic in town. If you have any problems with your car while here, he's your man. Kirby is James Gordan's nephew. He's a detective down in St. Petersburg," Charley said, turning toward his brother.

The big man shook his hand. "Sure, I can see a slight resemblance. Your uncle was a good friend of mine. I took care of his vehicles for years. I was sorry to learn of his death. He was a good man and a credit to this community."

"Thank you, Dean. Being separated by several states, I didn't get to spend nearly as much time with him as I would've liked. You're right though, he was a good man. He's been good to me and my sister."

"You going to be in town long?" Dean asked.

"I don't know, Dean. I've still got some loose ends to tie down, so I suppose I'll be around for a while. Who knows, I might even decide to dig in and call it home." Kirby's remark drew a quick glance from Amos.

"Maybe if he stays, you could find a place for him with the police department, Charley. He would need a job, you know." Amos chuckled.

"Always need good policemen, especially those with detective experience," Charley responded. "Incidentally, doesn't the Reece gal do some work for you folks?"

"You mean Connie Reece?" Amos asked.

"That's the one," Charley told him. "While she and her mother were walking out at Manning Mill just before dark last night, someone took a shot at them."

"Are they okay? Was either hurt?" Kirby quickly asked.

"Mrs. Reece is a little bruised from the fall she took during the incident, but both escaped without any real injury. It seems their dog ran the shooter away before he could get off more than one shot," Charley told them.

"What was the reason behind the shooting?" Kirby asked.

"So far we haven't been able to determine that. They've had no problems with anyone. The nature of the incident would seem to rule out robbery or sexual attack. So far, we've not been able to find even a hint of a motive."

Kirby's face suddenly took on a distant look. He was silent for a moment as if in deep thought. "It may have nothing to do with this," he finally said, "but do you remember the break-in we had in which some file folders were stolen? According to my sister, Connie's name was written on the inside of several of the folders identifying her as the researcher. It seems a little far-fetched to me, but maybe whoever took the shot was also Uncle James's murderer," Kirby reasoned.

"Yeah, I see where you're going. Maybe the shooter figured that since Connie did some research for your uncle, the two of them knew something he didn't want anyone to know. So, he decided to eliminate them. It's certainly worth looking into. I may want to talk with your sister about the content of those files," Charley suggested.

"Give me a call when you're ready to come by, or we can come to your office. I'm sure she will be more than happy to talk with you."

"If it's okay with you, I think I'll drive by there. I've been wanting to see what your uncle did with that old church building. I'll give you a call."

****

When Amos and Kirby got home, Amos immediately shared with Carol and Riley the news of the shooting escapade the Reece mother and daughter had endured the previous evening. "What's this world coming to when two sweet ladies can't even go out to walk their dog?" Carol lamented. "And you don't know who was responsible or why? You should have gone on down to the barber shop and gotten the rest of the story," she taunted her husband. "I'm going to make a big pot of vegetable soup, and you and I will take it to Beth and Connie," she announced, looking in Riley's direction.

"Carol thinks vegetable soup solves all problems," Amos remarked for the benefit of the two-younger people in the room.

While Carol was preparing soup and Amos was fiddling with something outside, Kirby and Riley retreated to Riley's apartment. They sat down at her kitchen table. "Chief Nelson plans to call and make an appointment to come by to talk with you about the content of the folders that were stolen. Do you remember what folders you pulled besides the ones I told you to look for?" he asked.

"It was just a few filed under the "local interest" tab. I never looked at the content. I was too absorbed in the others. I intended to eventually go through them to satisfy my personal curiosity about some of the history of the town. Most, if not all, had to do with unsolved local mysteries. I think Uncle James had a thriving curiosity about such matters—one about the murder of a government revenue man, others concerning a fire in the school, a bank robbery in Kingston, and the disappearance of a young woman. There were two or three others, but I don't remember what they were."

"You're always telling me what a keen memory you have. You might think about it and try to remember anything else before you talk with Chief Nelson. Do you remember if Connie was identified in those local mystery folders as researcher?"

"I don't remember if that was true of all the folders, but definitely in some of them. I think I see what you're thinking. You're considering the possibility that there might be a connection between Uncle James's death, our break-in, and the attempt on Connie Reece's life. You're assuming that Uncle James was murdered because he knew something someone didn't want him to know. Then, retrieving the folders, that person discovered that Connie was the researcher, meaning she also had knowledge of whatever it happened to be. So, he tried to kill her as well."

"I'm not assuming anything, but that's a possibility," Kirby answered.

"If that were the case, then why did the thief take all the folders on the desk?" Riley asked.

"Maybe he came looking for the one file that concerned him. Finding it on the desk with others, he took all of them so it wouldn't be apparent which one he was after. It may have been simply a precaution to cover his tracks."

"I can see that." Riley nodded in agreement. "It makes sense."

"I know it all looks logical, but even in my short career as a detective, I've already had cases I was sure I had completely figured out, only to discover later that I was totally off track. So, I don't assume anything. You do know what it means if, indeed, we are moving in the right direction?" Kirby asked. "It means you could be in danger. Whoever is responsible could assume you read the material that involves him, possibly causing him to go after you."

Kirby noticed Riley didn't look bothered much by that possibility. "Riley, you need to listen to me. Be careful! Whoever's behind this obviously is dangerous. His actions at the park last night tell me he's not a professional, but he's dangerous. *You need to be careful.*"

"I'm not concerned. I've got a big brother and a band of angels taking care of me. Do you think Earl Lance, the man with the missing twenty years, could be the guilty person?" Riley asked.

"I think that's a real possibility. If he thought Uncle James and Connie's research revealed something sinister about those years that could send him to prison, he could be the culprit."

"But I read his file and I saw nothing like that. I looked over the escape convict file and saw nothing that would tie him to anything other than a prison break," Riley told her brother.

"Maybe there's something there you missed, or maybe he just thought there was something in the file that would incriminate him. I'm glad you remembered his address. Tomorrow I plan to drive to Rome to have a talk with Mr. Earl Lance."

It was a while before Carol's soup was ready, but she and Riley did deliver it in time for the Reece ladies to have it for dinner along with Carol's delicious southern cornbread with no sugar. "The sugar belongs in the tea, not the cornbread," she emphatically declared before they left home. Riley came home telling Kirby all about their visit. Obviously, Riley had found a new friend, one to whom she felt she could relate. He was glad because she was accustomed to having friends in her own age bracket. Once she started law school, there would be many. He knew that because Riley, unlike himself, had a knack for gathering friends around her who adored her. A good friend now, here in Adairsville, would certainly make the adjustment easier for her. Besides, he decided, it wouldn't be a bad thing to have Connie around some. He thought he might like having the feisty young lady as his friend as well. Any girl who loved baseball was potentially his friend.

Kirby tried to concentrate on what he knew of the murder of his uncle and now the attack on the Reece ladies. Was there indeed a connection? But soon his mind went back to the Boston area with he and Sherrie walking on a Cape Cod beach on a Saturday just before sunset. He remembered the little church they attended the next day and how peaceful it all seemed. *The happiest time of my life,* he decided. He doubted he would ever experience such joy again. He slept very little.

CHAPTER 11

Kirby insisted on buying Amos breakfast, so they left home early. Amos recommended Shoney's near Cartersville which offers a breakfast buffet. "They have just about anything you could want on the buffet bar," Amos informed his companion. A few minutes later he proceeded to demonstrate that, even as a small man, he could put the biscuits and gravy away with the best of them. "I'm glad you suggested we visit a couple of our hardware stores before we look up this Lance in Rome," Kirby told Amos. "I don't know much about hardware, but if we decide to hold onto those businesses, I need to learn."

"Is that your plan?" Amos asked. "To keep the stores?"

"Riley and I have discussed it some. We're leaning that way since, according to the reports you've given us, each seems to be holding its own with profits. I guess the final decision hinges on getting to know the staffs and feeling confident we can trust them without having to micro-manage. We have decided to hold on to the rental properties including the apartment complex. I think we would be foolish not to. They produce solid income and since you've agreed to manage them, we really can't lose."

"You'll enjoy meeting Edwin Lumpkin and his staff at the store in Rockmart. There're good people. It's one of the first stores James acquired. From there, we'll visit the one in Lindale and then move on to Rome. It's just twenty-five or so miles home from there—a tidy little circle," Amos told him.

In less than a half hour after leaving Shoney's, they were in the Rockmart store. Kirby felt a little foolish trying to evaluate the enterprise with so little knowledge about the nature of the hardware business or even business in general, but he felt he knew something about people and that was his most important concern. Amos was right. He was impressed with Edwin Lumpkin and his staff. He left convinced this one would be an asset. The store in Lindale wasn't as impressive, with a less visible location, but he found no reason to be concerned about it. "As you know, this store is smaller in a smaller community. It's less profitable, but nevertheless, extremely important to the community. Without it, Lindale residents would have to drive out of town for their hardware needs," Amos told him. He went on to inform him of Lindale's history as a mill village. "You, being a former professional baseball player, will be interested in knowing the mill here had one of the better baseball teams in the old North Georgia Industrial League back in the 1940s and into the fifties. They tell me it wasn't unusual to see two or three thousand people cheering on their favorite team on a Sunday afternoon. Several of the star players, like Willard Nixon, who later pitched for the Red Sox, performed for the Lindale team.

"I've heard that name," Kirby replied. "I believe he was known as the 'Yankee killer' because of his uncanny ability to beat the New York Yankees."

"That's him," Amos confirmed. "After his major league career, he came back home and spent the remainder of his life here. I used to see him from time to time officiating high school basketball when I was going to some games."

During the remaining few miles to Rome, the two men discussed the Freddy Seals problem. They agreed they needed to settle the matter immediately. "I think I know your answer but let me ask again. "Are you certain there's nothing to his claim?" Kirby asked.

"I would bet the family farm on it," Amos responded. "If the family had a farm. I don't know that James was even acquainted with Freddy's mother, and I'm sure there was never a relationship between the two. Believe me when I tell you I would have known if there was anything to it."

"Then we need to get in touch with Seals as soon as possible, insist on a DNA report, and put this silliness to rest. I don't believe we should give in and offer him anything to go away. I suspect that's what he's hoping for," Kirby speculated. "Very likely he'll refuse the DNA test, but that's okay. He can't hurt us nor Uncle James's reputation if he refuses to cooperate."

"Do you think he had anything to do with James's murder?" Amos asked.

"At this point, I'm not ruling it out, but I've a hard time believing anyone could be so mentally flawed as to take a life to pull off a scam that has almost no chance of succeeding. I know this boy isn't the brightest bulb in the store, but it's hard to believe anyone could be that dumb."

"You haven't met this kid yet," Amos responded.

"That's why I'm withholding final judgment. I'm learning not to jump to conclusions. Looking forward to meeting the boy. Do you have any idea where 146 Mason Lane is?" Kirby asked, realizing they were approaching Rome.

"Carol and I lived in Rome when we were newlyweds. If I'm not mistaken, it's over in North Rome near where we lived." With Amos's directions, they were soon turning onto Mason where the low- to middle-income houses appeared to have been built in the 1950s or sixties. Kirby guessed most were rentals.

"There it is." Amos pointed to the right at a white frame house sitting back a little farther than some of the others.

Kirby whipped into the driveway, barely avoiding driving past it. "I don't see a car. Looks like no one's home," Kirby observed. "But we won't know for sure until we go and check it out." Walking toward the front door, Kirby noticed there were no curtains on the front windows. A glance inside revealed there wasn't furniture in the front room. "Well Amos, looks like we've done what I did often in my baseball career. We've struck out. I don't believe anyone is living here."

Kirby rang the doorbell several times with no response. "I noticed a lady next door who seems to be interested in what we're doing. She's watching us carefully from one of her windows. She might be able to give us some information," Amos suggested.

"Good idea," Kirby remarked as they walked across the yard to the door of the house where Amos had seen the woman at the window.

"Hi," Kirby said to the middle-aged lady who opened the door. "I'm Kirby Gordan. I'm a policeman from Florida," he told her, flashing his credentials. "This is my friend Amos Edwards. We're looking for Earl Lance. We were led to believe we could find him next door, but we didn't find anyone at home."

"You missed him by about a month," she told them. "He and Barbara, his wife, moved away about four weeks ago. It took us by surprise. We looked out one day to see them loading one of those big rental trucks."

"How long had they lived there?" Kirby asked.

"They were there for three or four years, longer than most of the neighbors we've had in the twenty-seven years we've lived here. Good neighbors too. Hated to see them go."

"Do you have any idea where they went?" Kirby inquired.

"I don't have an address, but they told us it was local. They didn't leave Rome."

"I assume they were renters; do you know who owns the house?" Kirby asked.

"Yeah, they rented, like just about everybody else in this neighborhood. We're among the few who own our house, or soon will," she added. "The people who own that house and a couple others on this street live in Florida, but Harris Realty manages their properties."

"One last question and we'll leave you alone. Do you have any idea what Mr. Lance does for a living?"

"Ever since we've known him, he's been a veterinarian's assistant. He first worked for a doctor in Shannon and then a year or two ago, he changed jobs. I believe Doctor Burnham is the name of his new boss. I think he's located near the little community of Plainville. But, as much as Earl loved animals, he was always looking around for something else. He complained a vet's assistant didn't make a whole lot of money."

"Thank you, ma'am," Kirby said to the lady as they were walking away. "You've been a great help."

"What now?" Amos asked when they got back to the car.

"Maybe we need first to go by Harris Realty to inquire about a new address for the Lances," Kirby suggested.

"Evidently, Lance once applied to James for a job. Did you ever meet him?" Kirby asked Amos as they drove to North Broad Street where Harris Realty was located.

"You know, I've been thinking about that. I'd forgotten about it, but I think James did introduce me to him. Maybe we even talked briefly. When you get to be my age, your memory is not as good as it used to be, but I'm pretty sure I met him. I think James was considering him for manager of the Summerville store."

The two men found no help from the lady behind the desk at Harris Realty. When Kirby asked about a forwarding address, the blond lady went to her files, but came back to tell them, "We have no forwarding address for Earl Lance, but if you're in the market, we can sell you a house."

"No, thank you ma'am. I already own houses I've never laid eyes on."

The lady looked at him rather strangely and then said, "We're also good at selling them."

Kirby smiled and kept walking out of the building toward the parked car. "Do you know how to get to Plainville?" Kirby asked. "Maybe we need to see if we can get information from Dr. Burnham's office."

"We can easily do that. A detour to Plainville will take us only a couple of miles out of the way," Amos informed him.

"Then that's what we'll do."

In fifteen minutes, before reaching Plainville, they saw a building with a sign standing out front that read "Burnham's Veterinary Clinic." They entered the building where they found a young lady and a man, obviously the doctor, going through a pile of papers on a desk.

"Dr. Burnham?" Kirby asked. "I'm Kirby Gordan, and this is Amos Edwards. We're looking for Earl Lance. We were told he worked here."

"Yes, Earl works here. He's not around right now. I own some cattle, and part of his job is to help me take care of my livestock. He's with about fifty-head in a pasture just across that field." The doctor pointed east. "He'll probably be back in thirty to forty-five minutes if you want to wait. If you'd rather, I have no objection to your walking over to the pasture where he's working."

"That sounds like a great idea. I need a little exercise," Kirby said, thinking it would be best to speak to Lance away from the other people in the office.

"Just keep walking in that direction." The doctor again pointed east. "Look for a herd of Herefords or a black Jeep Wrangler. That's what Earl drives. You'll find him nearby."

"The question is, do you know what a Hereford looks like?" Kirby asked Amos as they were strolling across the field.

"You really are a city boy, aren't you?" Amos answered. "I won't have any problems recognizing a herd of Herefords. What questions do you plan to ask Mr. Lance? You can't walk up to someone and ask, 'Are you that guy who escaped thirty years ago?' can you? Or maybe, 'Did you kill James Gordan?'"

"We may get around to those questions, but we'll start with less threatening ones and see where they lead."

They worked their way to the side of the field to continue their hike on a little farm road running between the open field and a stand of timber with a small stream between the woods and the road. "I know such investigations are old hat to you, but it's all new territory for me. I find it fascinating, but also a little intimidating. You know what they say about old dogs and new tricks."

"You may be learning some new tricks, but I certainly wouldn't call you an old dog."

"You wouldn't, would you? Son, I'm approaching seventy years of age. How long does a dog have to live in your part of the world before he's old?"

"I've known some people who were old at seventy, and I've known a few extremely young seventy-year olds. It didn't take me long to figure out that you're one of the young ones," Kirby told his companion.

"I wish you would tell my wife that. I guess you've noticed lately that she's gone to using Old Man as her pet name for me. I'm not sure I like that," Amos added.

Kirby laughed. "Maybe, if you started calling her Old Woman . . ."

At that moment, Kirby's voice stopped in mid-sentence. He suddenly heard an engine humming. His eyes turned to the left to see a Jeep come out of the woods a short distance in front of them. It moved toward them with accelerating speed. "Look out Amos!" Kirby cried out before diving onto the level ground to his right to avoid the vehicle. He saw Amos go to the ground hard on the opposite side of the road before rolling down the little hill toward the creek below. Kirby heard a splash and a loud *"Oh!"*

CHAPTER 12

Always the cop, even as Kirby was picking himself up off the ground, he was studying the license plate on the Jeep, trying to plant the letters and numbers in his mind. He ran across the little road, skidding down the hill to find Amos crawling out of the shallow stream, water and black muck dripping off his clothes. "It's a good thing I'm one of those young dogs. That could have killed an old one," Amos said, looking toward Kirby with a solemn expression. Then he broke into a booming laugh.

"It's not something to take lightly; you could've been killed."

"Don't take everything so seriously, my boy. I'm all right. The cold water was refreshing on a hot afternoon like we have today."

Kirby couldn't help himself. He joined his good-humored friend in chuckling at the odd situation in which they found themselves.

"Who would have thought that before we got home, you would take time out for a swim?" Kirby said, taking Amos's right arm to help him out of the shallow creek. "One thing is for sure: Earl Lance has no desire to talk with us."

Back in the parking lot, Kirby took a quick look around and saw no Jeep. "He's out of here," Kirby said. "We might as well head back to Adairsville. I'll drop you off at home so you can get into some dry clothes before I go by the station to report this to the chief. I think he might be interested in what happened here today."

A half-hour later, Kirby, sitting in front of the police chief's desk, told Charley Nelson the whole story of his suspicions about Earl Lance along with a review of the events of the day. "I've written down the license plate number of the Jeep he was driving," he said, handing a small piece of paper across the desk to the young chief. "I realize you probably have no reason to hold him for anything yet, but I think there's a chance he is a fugitive who's been able to elude justice for more than thirty years. I know it sounds a little crazy, but Uncle James may be dead because he figured that out. He's running from us for some reason. I think he might have reacted today as he did because he recognized Amos as Uncle James's associate. Amos said he only briefly met the man sometime back. He remembers almost nothing about him. But if Lance is a fugitive who's been running free that long, he's probably a rather observant and careful man. It's not beyond reason to believe he recognized Amos and figured it best to run."

"I certainly think it needs to be looked into," Chief Nelson stated. "I haven't said much to you about letting us do the investigating, because I think you're a lot like me. It's not going to do a lot of good to try to tell you anything. But I will remind you that whoever killed your uncle is dangerous. You, no matter how capable you happen to be, are putting yourself in harm's way by pursuing this alone. Let me suggest—no, let me insist—that if you keep poking around, take every precaution and keep my number on speed dial. I would have hated you coming by today to tell me my good friend Amos had been killed by a maniac in a Jeep."

"I know it's your duty to tell me that, and I understand what you're saying. I promise you I'll be careful and will do my best to stay out of your way."

"And keep me informed. I thank you for sharing with me today. Incidentally, I appreciated the talk I had with your sister earlier. She's a bright girl. She's going to be a good lawyer."

"Yes, she is. I've often suspected she's the brightest star in the Gordan family collection. So, you're up to speed on the content of the stolen files?"

"I think so," Nelson replied.

"You don't mind me talking with Connie Reece about what she might remember putting into those files, do you?" Kirby asked.

"I don't see how that could create any problems for us," the chief told him. "If she's good with it, then go ahead."

Kirby left the station thinking that it would be good to see again the perky girl he met a few days earlier who liked baseball. He told himself his feelings had to do only with the case, but he knew better. When Kirby got home, he found Amos, now in a blue shirt and jeans, along with Carol tending to some bushes growing alongside the walls on the corner where their apartment was located. "What were you and my husband trying to prove? I don't want him skinny-dipping, but I'd rather he didn't go swimming in his clothes either. I told the old man he needs to stay away from steep inclines beside creeks," Carol said with a glint in her eye and a slight hint of laughter in her voice.

Looking toward Amos, Kirby saw an expression which he interpreted as a plea for him not to tell Carol the whole story. "Just some loose dirt along the edge of the creek," Kirby responded. "Not his fault."

He didn't miss the look of relief that came across Amos's face. "I wondered if you have Connie Reece's phone number," he asked Amos.

"Yes, I do, but I'm sure it's in that rolodex sitting on the desk in the study. James, though he was learning, never much took to the electronic craze. He still kept phone numbers he would likely use there on his desk."

"Great," Kirby responded and then turned to go inside. He caught the look Carol gave her husband, causing him to add, "Just need to talk with her about what she put in those files that were stolen."

Kirby went into the study. The lights behind the stained-glass window, as always, were bright and made the window beautiful. He turned on the overhead lights, took his phone from his pocket and sat down at the desk to reach for the rolodex sitting in the middle of the desk. He flipped through the tabs till he found "Reece." Kirby then turned his chair around to admire the beautiful shepherd window. He sat for a few moments, allowing its beauty to sink in before starting to punch numbers on his phone.

"Connie, this is Kirby Gordan. I trust you and your mother are doing well after your recent ordeal at the park."

"I'm fine, and I think Mom is finally about over the soreness she had from her fall with me landing on top of her. We're just sitting around waiting for what comes next."

"I'm glad to hear that. I need to talk with you about some of the information you compiled for Uncle James. I was wondering if maybe we could get together for dinner tonight. That would give us the opportunity to talk business as well as get to know each other a little better."

There was a moment of silence on the other end of the line before Kirby again heard Connie's voice. "It's a little late to be making plans for tonight, but I suppose I could manage if we made it seven o'clock or later."

"We can do that. I'm sorry I didn't call earlier, but I've been tied up all day, and just got home in the last few minutes to get your number. I know nothing about local restaurants. Do you have any suggestions?"

"The Adairsville Inn is always a good choice."

"The Adairsville Inn it is. I'll come by for you at seven o'clock," Kirby told her.

"Why don't I meet you at the inn at seven?" Connie suggested.

"That'll work," Kirby responded. "I'll see you there."

Kirby wished he had gotten her number and made the call earlier. He had the feeling she didn't appreciate being a last-minute date or even being his date at all. He would do his best to make a better impression at the restaurant. He showered and shaved for the second time that day, put on a blue shirt with a pair of khakis and sat down to wait the hour and a half left until seven o'clock.

Kirby's thoughts went to some of the good times he and Sherrie had while still in their teens. He dozed off. In his dreams, he was again a baseball player and Sherrie a happy wife. She was floating around their little apartment like a butterfly. She laughed often as he remembered she had done in the early days of their marriage. Then the laughter turned to sadness, then weeping, and finally angry yelling that would not stop. He didn't know what to do to stop the incessant shouting. Why couldn't she be happy? Why could he no longer make her happy? He loved her. Why could she not love him?

Kirby awakened in a cold sweat, enough to cause him to feel dampness from his T-shirt beneath his favorite shirt. He rubbed his eyes before looking across the room at the clock on a nearby table. He saw it was twelve minutes past seven.

Oh no, so much for making a good impression. I'm already twelve minutes late. I need to take another shower, but there's no time. Kirby hurried through the front door toward his car. *She's probably on her way home by now!*

****

Connie looked at the clock on the wall of the small lobby at the Adairsville Inn and noted that Mr. Deep Pockets was now almost fifteen minutes late. She would give him five more minutes before she went home and made herself a peanut butter sandwich. *Who does he think he is? I don't care if he has his own yacht; he can't treat me this way. Besides, he played for the bottom-of-the-barrel teams in the Kansas City organization, not the New York Yankees.*

"You get stood up, Connie?" The irritated young woman turned to see Logan Freeman, who she had dated a few times while in high school. He was standing beside the girl who was obviously his date for the evening. Logan was grinning at her. It took her a moment to realize the date was Sheila Rittman. Sheila was about her own age, but she didn't know her well since she had gone to high school at Darlington, the private school in neighboring Rome. Her first thought was, *I'm surprised Mr. Rittman let her go out with Logan. He's got a smaller bank account and less standing in the community than even me.*

"It's beginning to look that way," Connie responded to her friend. At almost that precise moment, a somewhat rumpled Kirby came rushing through the door.

"I'm so sorry," he immediately declared when he spotted Connie. "I fell asleep and didn't wake until after seven o'clock."

Probably hadn't gotten his fourteen hours of sleep today, Connie silently reasoned.

"I don't believe I know your friend," Logan said, taking hold of Sheila's left arm as if to protect her from Kirby.

"Logan, this is Kirby Gordan. Kirby, this is Logan Freeman and his friend Sheila Rittman. I've known Logan all my life. He and I were in first grade together."

"Oh yeah, I know who you are. You're old man Gordan's nephew. The one who recently came into all that money."

"Yes, he's Mr. James Gordan's nephew. He's a police detective who lives in Florida," Connie, embarrassed, said to her clearly unsophisticated friend while giving him a disapproving look.

"Good to meet you, Gordan." Logan held his hand out. Kirby took it.

"Great to see you again, Kirby," Sheila said as she smiled at him and lightly placed her hand on his arm.

"You two know each other?" Logan asked.

"We're old friends," Sheila answered.

A perfect match, Connie decided.

"We met briefly the other day," Kirby quickly inserted.

The couple was seated at a table in the main dining room. "What's good here?" Kirby asked, opening the menu.

"Just about everything. I especially like the roast beef. It's basically just good southern cooking," she answered. "But maybe that's not your preference since you're from up north."

"I love southern food. Yes, I've spent much of my life in the eastern part of the country, but you need to remember my family roots are right here in Adairsville. My mother was an accomplished southern cook. She made the best fried chicken and mashed potatoes you ever ate."

"Then maybe you'd enjoy the fried chicken they serve here," Connie suggested.

"No, I'll try it another time. I think I'll take your suggestion and have the roast beef tonight."

"So, you mentioned the other day that you're trying to find a permanent position; what kind of job are you looking for?" Kirby asked her after the waitress took their order and disappeared.

"I'm not sure. My degree is in general business. I know I want something challenging. A secretarial position would bore me to tears. I'll be picky for a while, but if nothing that appeals to me opens, I will probably settle and take what I can get. I'm able to stay afloat now by doing short-term projects for people who know me and appreciate my ability. I know I can't spend the rest of my life expecting to make ends meet that way."

"Do you know what part of the country you want to settle in?" Kirby asked.

"If I had my preference, it would be somewhere in good ole Georgia, but I'm willing to consider other southern locations such as Tennessee or one of the Carolinas. I might even be open to the idea of moving to Florida."

"What if you got a great job offer in Indiana or Ohio or, perish the thought, New York City? Would you consider such an offer?"

"It would have to be something special. I'm sure you could detect, even if you weren't a detective, that I'm a southern girl through and through. I would like to stay right here in Adairsville, but that's not going to happen."

"Why do you say that?"

"Well, there are no real opportunities here for a girl like me."

"What do you mean, 'for a girl like you'? From what I see, you're bright, educated, ambitious and uh . . . beautiful," Kirby said. "And besides, you're a baseball fan. There must be opportunities for a young lady like that."

"Thank you for saying so," Connie responded looking down, with her face turning a little red. "I don't want this to sound conceited, but, you see, that's the problem. There're few positions open here for a girl with ambition."

"I see where you're coming from," Kirby responded. "Did you ever think about starting your own business?"

"I have, but the problem with that is it takes capital. Mom and I get by, but that's about it."

"So, you don't think you could be happy to fall in love and marry a nice guy right here in Adairsville and settle down as a wife and mother?"

"I think I would if it were the right guy, but to be truthful, I don't think I've met anyone yet who comes close to fitting the bill. For one thing, he would have to be secure enough to let me be myself. I don't think I could live the rest of my life letting someone else call all the shots for me."

"I understand. I remember some of my dad's sermons on marriage. He always said it was a team effort. Yes, he felt it was the husband's responsibility to be head of the family, but the husband is also to love his wife. I think that rules out him being dictator over his family. Dad always said the husband's leadership is to be guided by his love for his family."

"And what about you? You've told me what your father said, but what about you?"

"Oh, I pretty much agree with him. I saw him demonstrate what he taught every day in our family and I don't think anyone could have had a better marriage than him and Mom. He showed me the practical side of what he preached," Kirby concluded.

If he's got all the answers, then what happened in his first marriage? Connie wondered.

"Dinner is served," the waitress remarked as she began to take food off the large tray and place it on the table in front of them.

Connie was glad to see the waitress since she was not comfortable with the direction the conversation with this near-stranger had taken. She was somewhat surprised, however, to find him a much deeper person than she had earlier judged him to be. "You mentioned on the phone that you had questions about something I did for Mr. Gordan," Connie said as the waitress was leaving the table.

"Yes, I was wondering what you remembered about the escaped prisoner incident from thirty years ago. That information was in one of the stolen files. It might be specifically what the burglar was after. Do you remember anything about the man or the escape that might be helpful?"

"All I remember is what I told you the other day. I think he was nineteen years old. He had killed someone in a hit-and-run and was on his way back to the Chattanooga area to face the consequences. Right now, I can't even remember his name. There was some speculation that a girlfriend might have aided him in getting away, but nothing was ever proven. I believe her name was Barbara something. I don't remember the last name."

"Did you say 'Barbara'?" Kirby raised his head to look her straight in the eyes.

"Yes, I think that's right. Is it important?"

"It could be. Would you do me a favor? Would you go back and redo the research on that incident? Find everything you can find about the man and the escape. I'll be happy to pay you for your trouble."

"Sure. I can do that. Do you think this man has something to do with the break-in at your place, the shot at mom and me, or the death of your Uncle James?"

"There could be a connection between all, some, or none. Just looking at all the possibilities."

The remainder of the evening was given to getting acquainted. Connie was surprised to realize she was starting to like this guy she had predetermined would be placed low on her worst dates list. He was different than she had expected.

Connie's phone rang. She took it from her purse and looked at it. "I'd better take that. It's Mom. Hello Mom. Yes, I hear you. Calm down and tell me what happened." Connie was silent for a minute or two as she listened with a concerned look on her face. "Are you okay? Have you called the police? I'll be there in five minutes."

"Mom's had a break-in. I couldn't get a lot out of her. It's unlike her to be so beside herself. I'd better get home as quickly as I can." Connie was already moving toward the exit.

"I'll pay the bill and be right behind you," Kirby called out as he hurried toward the checkout counter.

CHAPTER 13

When Kirby arrived at the Reece house, Beth was sitting on the sofa with Connie beside her holding her hands. She was nervously telling the two policemen about the frightening experience she had just endured. "I heard a noise in the garage and thought maybe a cat or some other animal had gotten locked in. I went to the kitchen door that opens into the garage. I immediately saw the door on the other side of the garage, which we always keep locked, was standing wide open. I flipped the light switch, looked around, and saw nothing else out of the ordinary. But when I got to the open door, I saw someone running. He was already across the yard and just entering the woods. I saw he had something in his left hand, and it didn't take me long to realize it was a gun."

"Was it a rifle or a handgun?" one of the policemen asked.

"It was a rifle," the distraught victim immediately replied.

"Did you see which way he went when he entered the woods?" the second policeman probed.

"No, it was dark, and those woods are dense. He just disappeared when he got to that point."

"What was he wearing?" the first officer asked.

"It looked like he was dressed in all black, I guess it could've been navy blue or some other dark color. I could tell he had a ski mask over his head."

"We're going to walk out to the edge of the woods to take a look," one of the uniformed policemen told them. "Mrs. Reece, would you point out for us approximately where the prowler entered the woods? And while we are out there, would you ladies look around the garage to see if anything is missing?"

Beth walked with the two policemen to the door that had been found open earlier. She pointed toward a peach tree she had planted several years earlier on the edge of the yard and told them, "That's where he left the yard, just right of the peach tree."

Beth and Connie, accompanied by Kirby, walked around the garage, giving careful attention to the contents, consisting mostly of gardening and lawn tools. "I don't see anything missing, do you?" Connie asked her mother.

"No, I don't."

"You must have scared him away before he could take whatever he was after," Connie suggested.

"Or he couldn't find anything worth stealing," Beth said with a nervous laugh.

Kirby said nothing, but he was almost sure the intruder had not been there to steal something. The previous event in the park, and the fact the masked man was carrying a rifle, led him to believe he meant to do either Connie or Beth harm. Most petty thieves don't carry rifles. If they have a gun, it's usually a handgun. His guess was that when the trespasser entered the garage, he saw Connie's car was missing, and concluded she was not home. That's when he left. The intruder was probably after Connie. "What's on the other side of those woods?" Kirby asked Connie.

"The woods go back maybe a hundred yards, and then there's a street with houses that were built in the last year," she told him.

"You ladies don't need to be here alone. Is there someone you know who can come and stay with you?"

"I've already called my brother," Connie told him. "He'll be here shortly."

"Until this guy is caught, I don't want the two of you staying here alone at night. I know the police are patrolling regularly, but that guy got in tonight. He could do it again. If you get caught without another alternative, you can come stay with us. I'm sure

Riley would be pleased to have one of you as a guest and Amos and Carol will take the other," Kirby told her.

"We appreciate your concern and your offer, but we'll keep Robert here with us until this is resolved. Do you think this was the same guy who shot at us in the park?" Connie asked him with a concerned note to her voice.

"I can almost guarantee it," he told her. "The rifle, ski mask, dressed in dark clothing. It has to be the same man."

Kirby stayed with them until Robert, who was a couple years younger than Connie, arrived. He wasn't comfortable leaving the ladies' safety in the hands of one so young and inexperienced, but what could he do? "It takes me less than five minutes to get here from my place. You should have no qualms about calling, should you need me."

Kirby drove to the street on the other side of the woods after leaving the Reece home. He discovered that Connie was right. Few of the newly built houses were occupied. He found one house in the block directly behind Connie and Beth's house where there were lights. He stopped, got out, and rang the doorbell. A large man with a slice of pizza in his hand came to the door. "I'm Kirby Gordan, and I'm a policeman investigating a break-in at a house just on the other side of the woods behind you. I was wondering if you have seen any person or vehicle that you thought didn't belong here this evening." He flashed his credentials, hoping the gentleman didn't notice they were issued by a Florida department.

"Yes, as a matter of fact, when I came in a little over an hour ago, I noticed a car sitting in the driveway of the house two doors down. No one resides there, and there were no lights on in the house. I wondered about it."

"Did you notice what kind of car it was?"

"No, I'm not really good at identifying models of cars, but I did notice it was black and probably a newer model. I didn't stop to examine it closely, but the thought did run through my mind that it was probably an expensive car."

"Did you see anyone around the vehicle?"

"No one at all. Just what looked like an empty car sitting there," he responded.

"Thank you, sir. You've been helpful," he told the man who took a bite of the pizza in his hand before closing the door.

****

Riley had heard Kirby return home the previous evening, but she had not yet talked with him. She wondered how his date with Connie had gone. She hoped it went well. She liked the girl a lot. She would be good for Kirby. In the last couple of days, Connie noticed her brother had begun to take on a little more zest for life. She wasn't sure where it came from, but she suspected Connie might have something to do with it. Whatever the reason, she was thankful for progress.

Spending the day with Carol had her excited. Carol wanted to introduce her around town. They planned to visit some of the shops and have lunch at the Maggie Mae Tea Room at the 1902 Stock Exchange. They would also look for some new clothing for the three children of The Cleaning Crew. Hopefully, later in the day, they'd have an opportunity to deliver those purchases. Maybe they'd find something for the wives as well.

About to take a bite of the cream-cheese-covered bagel in her hand, Riley heard a knock at her door. It couldn't be Carol. It was still almost an hour before they planned to begin their excursion. She opened the door to find her brother with a big smile on his face.

"Well, from the looks of you, you must have enjoyed your date last night," she surmised.

"It wasn't really a date," Kirby declared. "We just got together for dinner to discuss some business. But, yes, I did enjoy our *business discussion*."

"She's a sweet girl, isn't she?" Riley asked, and then watched her brother's face for clues as he responded.

"I don't know if *sweet* is the word I would use. She's smart. She's motivated. She's opinionated. She's unique. She's sensitive. She's lovely, and I like her a lot."

"I just knew you would. I've been hoping the two of you would hit it off."

"Don't get too excited, sis. We've only gotten together for dinner one time. We haven't talked about marriage or anything like that. I'm not sure she even likes me."

"I know, but it's a start. That's all I was hoping for," she declared.

"I wanted to let you in on something else that happened last night," Kirby told her. "Connie got a call from her mother before we left the restaurant. Someone with a gun broke into their garage. Evidently, when he noticed Connie's car was not there, he ran away."

"So, he was after Connie," she guessed.

"Yes, that would seem to be the case. It also appears it was the same man who shot at them in the park. The police were called, but he got away. Her brother is, presently, staying with them. I told them if that didn't work out, they could stay with us until this is settled. I figured Connie could be your guest and Beth could stay with Amos and Carol. If that didn't work, they could stay in my apartment and I could sleep on your sofa. Would you see how Carol would feel about that, should it become necessary?"

"I'll talk with her, but I'm sure both she and Amos will be ready to help in any way they can."

"I thought so too. I sort of feel responsible for what's happening to them since I think it's somehow tied to her work for Uncle

James," Kirby explained. He ate one of Riley's bagels before returning to his own apartment and ultimately to the study.

When the two ladies started north on Interstate 75, Carol drove, and Riley relaxed on the passenger side. They would be to the Calhoun Outlet Mall in ten minutes. Riley had thought little about it until the last few days, but she had spent almost no time with women older than herself over the last four years. Perhaps that was why she so enjoyed time with Carol. That and the fact her new friend was so much fun. Riley decided there were several factors that drew her to this lady at least forty years her senior. Carol laughed easily, approached every task as if it was the most important job in the world, and she cared deeply about people. How could you not love and attach yourself to someone like that?

The two shoppers arrived at the mall just as most of the stores were opening their doors for the day. In the next two hours, they managed to spend time in three shops specializing in children's clothing, two that sold women's wear, and two shoe stores. Twice, they had to take packages to the car before they could continue their shopping spree. Carol even found a Sunday dress for herself.

"Success," Riley declared as they got into the car to head back toward Adairsville. "This should give the two school-age children the clothes they need to start school in the fall, and the little one will not feel left out either."

"I hope we guessed right on the ladies' sizes. I wonder how long it's been since those women have had new dresses," Carol commented.

"I'm sure it's been awhile," Riley replied. "If the sizes are wrong, we'll exchange them. I think we should stop by the apartments and deliver these items before we do the other things we've planned for the day."

"You can't wait for those children to get their new things, can you?" Carol commented, her eyes twinkling.

"I love seeing those little faces light up," Riley admitted.

They found all the ladies and children at home. Riley knew the three men were busy with a job in Cartersville. Upon receiving their new clothes, the eyes of the children did light up, while the ladies' eyes filled with tears. They shared some time together and there were embraces before they departed.

"Now it's on to beautiful downtown Adairsville," Carol announced.

"You make it sound like New York City, or maybe Chicago," Riley said, chuckling.

"Oh, it's better than those places," Carol declared. "Not as big, but better. I like many of the things big cities can provide, but I love the intimacy of a small town. I love walking down the street and knowing almost everyone I meet. I enjoy going into the shops where the visit is as much a social occasion as a business transaction. I like a town where people pretty much behave themselves because everyone knows them and what they're doing. I get a lot of pleasure from the colorful characters that are a part of a small town. I'm sure they're in cities too, but they get lost in the numbers. They can't hide in a small town and they keep life from getting boring."

The two ladies started on the north side of the street where they spent some time with the "other Carol" at the General Store & Mercantile. Both women left with small bags of merchandise they decided they couldn't live without. From there, they went to Elite Fashions, a little shop that offers ladies' fashions.

"This is the longest-continuing business on the street," Carol explained. "I've bought many of the clothes I've worn over the past thirty years right here at Elite. They've always got new things coming in. I try to check it out at least once every two or three weeks."

Down at the end of the street, they went into the 1902 Stock Exchange Building. "Actually, it's three buildings that hold several shops, including the used-and-rare bookshop run by our friend, Davis Morgan. The Adairsville Opera House, a dinner theater, is upstairs. One of the biggest draws is the Maggie Mae Tearoom, where we'll eat lunch today."

Once inside the 1902 Stock Exchange, they were met by a young clerk Carol introduced to her as Janie. Riley guessed the clerk with the deep southern accent wasn't much older than herself. She liked her immediately.

"I think we'll have some lunch before looking around," Carol told Janie, who escorted them to a table in the quaint tearoom. "You get whatever you want," Carol told her, "but the chicken salad is to die for. Amos likes the Reuben."

****

Back home, Kirby took some time out from studying files related to their hardware and lumber business to drive to nearby Zaxby's for carryout. He just had sat down to eat his chicken wings when he heard a knock at his door. It was Amos carrying his phone in his hand. "Come on in, Amos. I'll share my chicken wings with you," he offered.

"No, thanks," the older man said with an uncharacteristically serious look on his face. "I thought I needed to share this with you as soon as possible. I received this text five minutes ago." He handed Kirby his phone.

Kirby read the message: *Keeping an eye on that beautiful guest of yours. Wouldn't want anything to happen to her. Watched her go to Calhoun with your old lady this morning. Went into seven stores at the mall. Came back to visit with those no accounts you've taken under your wing. Went to General Mercantile, Elite, and are now sitting at a table inside the 1902 Stock Exchange where they both ordered chicken salad plates. You can see I'm watching her closely because it would be a shame if something like what happened to the old man would happen to her. Pay me what's due to me, and you've nothing to worry about. See you soon.*

"Is he crazy? He's threatening Riley and all but admits he murdered Uncle James. Obviously, he wants us to know who's behind it. It couldn't be anyone but Freddy Seals," Kirby declared. "Let's get to the 1902 Stock Exchange as quickly as we can. Maybe we can take care of this problem now."

Within two minutes they were in the car headed toward town. "I know you're upset that he threatened your sister but giving Freddy what he deserves is not the way to approach this. Any brutality will only get you in trouble."

"I know, Amos. You don't have to worry. As much as I would like to beat him to a pulp, that's not my way. I'll control myself."

"Hello handsome," the sugar-coated voice greeted them when they entered the Stock Exchange. Kirby turned to his right to look in the direction from which the voice came. He saw a young woman with a big grin was the source of the flirtatious expression.

"Oh, she's talking to me, not you," Amos declared with a smug look and a grin.

"How do you know that?" Kirby questioned.

"Because I'm the handsome one."

"Don't let him fool you. I call him that because he told me that was his first name," the young woman declared.

"Kirby, this is Janie. She works here and don't believe anything she tells you. Is my wife here, young lady?" Amos asked.

"She's in the tearoom enjoying lunch with Kirby's sister."

"How do you know it's Kirby's sister?"

"You know nothing gets past me, Amos. I'm all-knowing, as they say."

"Yeah, you don't miss any of the gossip that goes on in this place. Do you know Freddy Seals?"

"I know him. I wish I didn't. That worthless piece of . . ."

"Watch your language, Janie," Amos exhorted.

"You know I have to do that in here. That preacher back in the bookstore would wash my mouth out with soap if I said anything inappropriate. I was going to say, 'that worthless piece of trash.'"

"Even that's not nice for a lady to be saying. Has he been in today?" Amos asked.

"He was in here a little while ago pretending to be a customer, peeping around corners watching what was going on in the tearoom. About five minutes before you got here, I threatened to call Charley if he didn't get off the premises. I saw him leave in that beat-up old pickup he drives. Do you want to go in the dining room and be seated with your wife and the pretty lady?" Janie asked.

"No, we won't bother them. You don't need to tell them we were here," Amos instructed.

"Well, I guess we'll have to wait to confront our juvenile delinquent. Would you give him a call and set up an appointment with him?" Kirby asked shortly after they got into the car. "I think maybe we should drive down to the police station and show Chief Nelson that text on your phone. Now, Amos, tell me about Janie."

CHAPTER 14

"**D**o you have any idea why Freddy wants to meet us all the way out at Pine Log?" Kirby asked Amos as he drove east on Highway 140.

"I've no idea. When he called and said he wanted to see us, I told him to name the place since I didn't want him near the house. The cemetery beside the Methodist church in Pine Log was the location he gave me. It's a rather isolated spot. Maybe that has something to do with it."

"We may need to be on our toes. An irrational oddball like him can be dangerous. It's hard to figure what to expect from such a person. They don't think logically. I wouldn't rule out anything regarding him."

"Do you think he's James's murderer?" Amos asked.

"I don't know. He could be just enough off balance to think he could kill Uncle James, and then, claiming to be his son, come away with a huge inheritance. But it seems more likely to me when Uncle James died, Freddy saw an opportunity to try to get himself a good paycheck. But who knows with a washout like Freddy Seals? Tell me about this church and cemetery to which we're going," Kirby requested.

"It has quite a history." Amos immediately shifted into his familiar storytelling tone, or, as Carol calls it, his yarn mode. "The little church has been the primary place of worship for the people in that little community for well over 150 years. The cemetery on the hill beside the church is the burying place for just about everyone who expires in Pine Log. There is an old-fashioned campground on the premises that goes back to the mid-1800s. It's still used each year as the site for a week of camp meetings. There's a noteworthy story of an incident that happened there, I believe in

1886." Amos paused and leaned to the right as Kirby took a curve to the left a bid faster than Amos would've preferred.

Amos said nothing to Kirby about his speed but did give him a quick stare before continuing his history lesson. "A preacher by the name of Sullivan had been fervently preaching all week in the sweltering August heat, but nothing much was happening. The people were not responding. It was the last night of the meeting that the preacher fell to his knees and started praying, 'Lord, if it takes it to move the hearts of these people, shake the ground on which this old tabernacle stands.'

"They say the words were hardly out of his mouth when the building started shaking so forcefully that everyone in the building felt it. Some said the preacher's water pitcher and glass of water on the pulpit visibly shook. The reaction was immediate. The people started rushing to the front to pray. Soon even some who had not attended the meeting were making their way to the tabernacle. The meeting continued throughout the night with great results."

"You say that's a true story?" Kirby asked.

"As God is my witness, ever word of it is true."

"I guess sometimes it takes the ground moving beneath us to get us going in the right direction," Kirby remarked.

"You're right about that," Amos responded, looking closely at his young friend behind the wheel.

"I must add one footnote to the story. The next day the people were told there had been an earthquake in Charleston, South Carolina. It was shockwaves from that earthquake that shook the tabernacle at old Pine Log campground. Knowing that, however, didn't change anything as far as Pine Log people were concerned. They figured it was all the result of a prayer in Pine Log, and if the Almighty wanted to extend it to Charleston, that was His business."

"That's a great story," Kirby said as they drove into a spot beside the Pine Log Methodist Church. Makes one think." They got out and walked to the cemetery. "Looks like Freddy hasn't gotten here yet," he remarked.

"He's still got about eight minutes," Amos responded, looking at his watch. Eight minutes passed. Still Freddy was nowhere in sight. They walked through the cemetery, examining the inscriptions on some of the headstones. Fifteen minutes went by and still he had not arrived.

****

Riley was breathing hard when she entered the yard after her daily walk and run. When she heard an approaching engine, she turned her head to see an old beat-up pickup drive in behind her. She instantly recognized the truck. Freddy Seals was in the driver's seat. Riley started sprinting toward her door but having already jogged four miles, Freddy was out of the truck and caught her before she could get to the door.

"Where're your brave friends today?" Freddy screamed at her when from behind he wrapped both arms around her and started pulling her toward his truck.

"Help me," Riley called out and screamed a couple of times. Carol came out from her apartment. Upon seeing her, Freddy continued to keep one arm tightly around Riley while he opened the truck door and picked up a revolver off the seat. With his left hand he fired a shot in Carol's direction. She ducked back inside but continued to keep her head in a position to see what was going on. "Don't hurt her," Riley begged.

"Then you'd better stop your fighting and get into the truck," he demanded. He let go of her but continued to point the pistol in her direction. She got into the truck. Freddy held the gun in one hand and drove with the other. He hit the gas pedal, making the wheels squeal. He headed toward the highway, all the while laughing like a mad man.

"Where're you taking me?" Riley demanded.

"Somewhere where no one can find us," he told her. "Did you think you could hide from Fabulous Freddy?" the demented youth asked. "Freddy gets what he wants!"

Riley remembered her phone was in the pocket of her running shorts. She hoped it would not occur to Freddy that she might have a phone. Not being familiar with her surroundings, it was hard to keep track of where they were going, but she was determined she would be able to give someone directions, should she get the opportunity to use her phone. She tried to let it all register as they went north, away from downtown, until they turned left at a brick church with a cemetery on a hill on its westside. The cemetery had a flagpole beside the road. They went down a hill, across some railroad tracks, and across a bridge with a stream of water beneath. On the right, she saw a development with a sign on the road that identified it as Woody Farms. They drove at least three or four miles before taking a left. She could clearly see the sign that said, "Lancaster Road." The road curved in several places and they went up and down hills. Freddy then turned left into the remnants of a road where there had once been a house, but now only three outbuildings stood. Only one of those buildings looked substantial. Freddy stopped in front of that one.

"Get out," Freddy ordered Riley as he was exiting the driver's side, revolver still in hand. "You need to watch out for snakes," he told her. "Lots of snakes around here, and I hate snakes." He forced her to walk ahead of him into the building. He pointed her toward the end of the structure built with logs, thus sturdier than the rest of the building. She was placed in a room which he padlocked. "I've got some business to take care of, but I'll return soon, and maybe we can get to know each other better."

Riley heard his footsteps leaving the sorry excuse for a building. She would let him get far enough away that she could talk without his hearing before pulling out her phone.

****

Kirby and Amos gave Freddy almost a half-hour past the time they agreed on before they left Pine Log to start back to Adairsville. Almost back to town, Amos's phone made the sound that alerted him that a text was coming in. He pulled the phone out of his pocket. He was shocked at the message he was reading.

"Listen to this, Kirby: *I've got your girl, Riley. If you want her back, meet me at the Oothcaloga Cemetery at ten o'clock tomorrow morning with one hundred thousand dollars. If you don't show up with the money, she goes on a long trip with me.*"

"That's why Freddy wanted us in Pine Log. He wanted us out of the way so he could snatch Riley. I guess he decided getting the money he wanted by a more conventional scheme wasn't going to work. Tell him we'll be there with the money. And tell him this too: if he touches her, he'll regret it for the rest of his life."

Almost precisely the moment Amos put his phone back into his pocket, Kirby's phone rang. Since he was driving, Kirby handed it to Amos. "Hello, Kirby is occupied, this is Amos."

"I've got to talk quickly and keep my voice down, so listen closely. Freddy Seals has kidnapped me. I'm going to tell you where I am the best I can." Riley preceded to describe the route they took to get there. "We're in an old collapsing building to the left after the road takes a deep dip," she told him.

"I know exactly where you are. We'll be there in fifteen minutes or less," Amos responded. "Don't do anything to rile him. Stay safe until we get there."

"I'd better hang up. He's going to be back at any moment. There's no telling what he'll do if he catches me with this phone."

"Freddy does have her. She gave me directions to where they are. You need to continue straight ahead as fast as you dare."

"Call the police and tell them what's happened and where we are going," Kirby instructed before stomping on the accelerator. With nothing ahead of them, they were instantly exceeding ninety miles per hour.

"Carol called a few minutes ago to tell me about the kidnapping," Charley told Amos when he got him on the phone. "Evidently, he took a shot at Carol," he added.

"Is she all right?" Amos, now alarmed, abruptly asked the police chief.

"She's fine, Amos. Just shaken. She wasn't hit or harmed in any way."

"Riley let us know where they are. They went in on the end of the road where it's called Lancaster, but if you'll take the other end of the road off 140, it's called Big Ditch. Drive past the little cemetery on the right. The road curves and dips. They are in a dilapidated building to your right. Kirby and I are on our way there now."

"See you there. If you reach them before us, don't take any chances," Charley instructed.

****

Now that her eyes had adjusted to the semi-darkness in her place of confinement, Riley could dimly see her surroundings. Looking to her right, she was at first startled to see a snake on the floor. It didn't take her but a moment to identify the red and black medium-sized reptile as a king snake, a non-poisonous species she knew well. Riley had overcome any fear she had of snakes when a high school friend kept one as a pet. She often handled that one. One summer while in college, she volunteered two days a week in a zoo. There, she was exposed to reptiles on a regular basis. She heard Freddy returning. Remembering that he said he hated snakes, she quietly moved over to where the king snake was. She carefully picked it up with her fingers just below its head. She held the snake behind her back.

Freddy unlocked the door to enter the stall. He had the revolver stuck in his belt. "Now we're going to have a little fun," he said. "You may find out you like ole Freddy a lot more than you thought you did." He took another step toward her.

"You stay away from me," Riley demanded.

"What're you going to do if I don't?" He asked with a smirk and a laugh. He took another step toward her. He was now less than six feet away.

Riley moved her right hand with which she held the snake from behind her back so Freddy could clearly see what she had. He took a few steps backward when he realized she held a snake. "Throw that thing in the bushes," he demanded. She took two steps toward him.

"No, I won't," she firmly stated. "I know about snakes and this is one of the most poisonous species in this part of the country. If you take another step toward me, I'll throw him directly at you."

Freddy pulled the gun from his belt.

"Put that gun back in your belt, or I'll throw it in your face right now," she threatened. "You'll be dead in thirty minutes."

He put the gun back into his pants. "You're crazy. It takes a crazy person to hold a snake like that," he declared.

It occurred to Riley how ironic it sounded for him to call her crazy. The man's elevator obviously didn't go to the top floor. Deciding she had him on the run, she made the decision to try to take it a step further. "Lay that gun on the shelf to your left and step away from it."

"You're out of your mind if you think I'm going to do that," he resisted.

Riley took another step toward him and said, "Okay, you and this snake can fight it out then." She brought the snake back as if to throw it at him.

"No," Freddy screamed. "Keep that snake away from me."

When he pulled the gun from his waistband, Riley didn't know if he was going to use it to shoot her or lay it on the shelf. He laid it on the shelf. With snake still in hand, she breathed a sigh of relief before she took the few steps to where she could reach the shelf. She threw the snake in the corner away from her and Freddy before picking up the gun. She pointed it in Freddy's direction. "I'll not hesitate to use this if I have to," she told her captive.

"Okay, but let's get out of here. I don't want to be anywhere near that snake."

"That snake can't hurt you. He's no more poisonous than I am." She motioned for him to go through the door to the outside.

When they were back in the sunlight and away from the snake, Freddy perked up. "You could never kill anyone with that gun. You don't have the gumption to pull the trigger," he told her. "You're too sophisticated to do anything like that."

"You're right in saying that I couldn't kill anyone with this gun. I doubt if it's in me to take the life of another human being, but you're wrong in saying I won't pull the trigger. My brother is a policeman, and he taught me how to shoot. I'll protect myself. If you come toward me, I'll first shoot your right leg out from under you. If that doesn't do the job, I'll take out the left leg. If I must, I'll render both your shoulders useless. So, you had better stay right where you are. No, I won't intentionally take your life, but to protect myself, I will make things pretty miserable for you over the next few weeks."

Freddy looked at her face, probably trying to decide if she would do what she was threatening. Evidently, he believed her because he gave her no more trouble. Within five minutes Chief Nelson and three other officers, including two county sheriff's deputies, arrived in two cruisers to find Riley sitting on a large rock with a revolver in hand and Freddy on the ground a few feet in front of her.

"Looks like you didn't need us after all," Charley said to her. "I can't wait to hear how this happened." One of the officers, Mike, who Riley remembered from their earlier encounter, put hand-cuffs on Freddy and read him his rights. Kirby and Amos arrived a minute or two later, skidding to a halt before racing at almost a trot toward the group of people gathered beside the decaying old building.

"No reason to hurry," Charley told them. "Everything's under control."

Kirby embraced his sister, holding her tight for a couple of minutes before turning toward the chief. "Thank you, Charley, for getting to Riley in time."

"I had nothing to do with it. When I got here, Riley was sitting on a rock holding a gun on this punk. Your sister is one tough lady," Charley grinned.

"I've known that for a long time. No other like her." Kirby beamed and again pulled her close to him.

They stayed at the scene long enough for Chief Nelson to get the information he needed from Riley. "That's one fascinating girl," Riley overheard Mike tell the chief as she was leaving with Kirby and Amos.

That evening Kirby, Riley, Amos, and Carol gathered in the Edwards' dining room where they enjoyed a big pot of soup along with the wonderful cornbread Carol had prepared. When they reviewed the day, they counted their blessings. It was a rough day, but everyone came out unscathed.

"I'm sometimes amazed at how bad things can get without anyone getting seriously hurt," Amos remarked. "You would think there's someone up there taking care of us."

Before they got up from the table, Kirby surprised them all. "I think I'm going to church with you guys tomorrow. I've been on shaky ground long enough. Maybe I need to start finding my way back to that solid ground we were talking about earlier," he said, looking at Amos.

"Well, that's a good place to start," Amos told him, displaying a happy smile.

Riley's heart was deeply touched. *What a day it's been. I can't imagine what'll be next,* she thought before Amos's voice interrupted her thoughts.

"I think that young police officer, Mike, really likes you," he speculated as they started getting up from their seats.

"Oh, Amos, you said that before. He probably likes every girl he meets," Riley objected, while at the same time thinking, *maybe he does. And he's kind of cute.*

Her mind was so full of thoughts, it took Riley a long time to fall asleep that evening. Her prayers were filled with words of thanksgiving. Thanks for God's protection, even a little snake he sent her way. But most of all she thanked God for the words her brother had spoken at the dinner table. When she did sleep, she slept soundly.

CHAPTER 15

When Sunday morning came, the four casually but neatly dressed people took two cars. They parked side by side in the church parking lot and walked together to the stately brick building. Once inside, they seated themselves four rows from the back on the right side of the worship auditorium that appeared to Kirby to adequately seat around three hundred people. Kirby had been in the building at his uncle's memorial service but noticed little about the edifice on that occasion. Taking a more observant look today, he found the worship center to offer a quiet, dignified environment. Having grown up attending a series of traditional churches that his father pastored, that pleased him. Though Kirby had seldom attended services in recent years; he was aware of the present-day trend of constructing worship centers that looked more like theaters than churches. *That's okay if that's what appeals to the people who use such structures, but I think I'm more comfortable in a church that looks like those that meant so much to me in years past,* he thought.

It occurred to Kirby that this was the very church his father had attended as a youth. He knew it wasn't the same building. That place, where his father had been active in youth group and ultimately preached his first sermon, had been replaced by this one some years ago. That fact, however, did not distract from the warm feeling Kirby got from being in his dad's home church. He noticed several people he recognized. A group gathered around a couple with a baby. Everyone wanted to touch the infant, and there were smiles on all their faces. This had to be the first Sunday for Davis and Deidre's baby to be in church. Having met the couple, Kirby knew it would be the customary place for the child on Sundays for years to come and probably for the rest of his life.

Charley Nelson, dressed in civilian clothes, came in with a pretty lady Kirby assumed was the chief's wife. He heard someone refer to her as Tonya. They found a place several rows in front of where Kirby and his group were sitting.

"Hello, Amos." The greeting came from a well-dressed man with a deep voice that gave a slight hint of a southern twang. "I want to meet your guest."

"Preacher Jensen, this is Kirby Gordan. I believe you've met his sister, Riley."

"Yes, I have, and it's good to have you with us today, Kirby. You know, your dad is still somewhat of a hero among the people of this church. He was the first Timothy to go out from this flock and faithfully stick with the work to which he was called," the preacher told them.

"He's still my hero. He was the best man I ever knew," Kirby responded.

"You have a great heritage, a lot to live up to," Preacher Jensen reminded him.

"I guess I do," Kirby admitted. "I'm afraid I haven't always successfully done that, maybe I can do better in the future."

"That's the stuff! You're a man after my own heart. Please know I'm available to aid you in whatever way I can," the preacher assured him. And Kirby felt sure he meant it.

After the preacher moved away from them toward the front of the auditorium, Kirby looked around to see if he might find Connie and her mother in the crowd that had gathered but didn't see them. *Maybe they go to another church or perhaps they don't go to church at all.* That thought disturbed him until he recalled his own situation. Until today, he hadn't been in church in months. Who was he to judge anyone for their lack of church attendance?

Shortly after the worship leader had the congregation stand and the music started, Judson Rittman entered with his right arm in a sling. A lavishly dressed lady, presumably his wife, strolled pretentiously alongside the man. His daughter, Sheila, walked behind them. When she saw Kirby, she smiled in his direction. Kirby acknowledged her smile with a slight nod. Judson stopped a couple of times and used his left hand to shake the hand of someone he felt worthy of his attention before finally sitting on the second pew. Kirby, who had not given a great deal of attention to scripture recently, nevertheless recalled the words of Jesus in His sermon on the mount, words with which he had grown-up: *"And when you pray, do not be like the hypocrites, for they love to pray standing in the synagogues and on the street corners to be seen by men. I tell you the truth, they have received their reward in full."*

The well-planned service lasted just over an hour. Kirby liked the music and was impressed with the sermon by Clark Jensen. He began to lose his concentration and squirm a bit before the benediction was pronounced. *Nothing new,* he decided. *The truth is, I used to do that toward the end of Dad's sermons.* Kirby's mind went back to his teen years when he often sat with Sherrie at his side while his father presented his sermon. A familiar sadness overwhelmed him.

Several people introduced themselves to Kirby after the service. Chief Nelson ran him down before he reached the parking lot. "I know church is not the place to talk business, but I thought you might like to know that we have extensively questioned Freddy. He admits trying to con you people out of money and, of course, kidnapping Riley, but he vows and declares he had nothing to do with your uncle's death, the break-ins, or the attempt on the lives of the Reece ladies."

"Do you believe him?" Kirby asked.

"I don't know. He's capable of just about anything, but right now, we don't have any real evidence that he committed murder. Nevertheless, the kidnapping charge should get him off the streets for a long time. I'd better catch my wife before she gets to the car or I may be walking home." Charley was already hurriedly moving toward his car. "Good to have you in church with us to-day. Tonya and I want to have you and Riley for dinner sometime soon," he yelled back to Kirby. "It'll give us the opportunity to talk shop."

"Wait up, Gordan." Kirby heard a voice coming from behind him. "I want you to meet my wife."

Kirby turned to see Judson Rittman coming toward him with Sheila and Mrs. Rittman trailing behind. He and his companions stopped to wait for the group to catch up to them. "What did you do to your arm?" Kirby asked Rittman when the middle-aged man extended his left hand for the customary greeting.

"Oh, just a home repair injury. I fell off the ladder while do-ing some touchup painting. It seems my right shoulder took the worst of it. Nothing serious though. It's just a small fracture, hardly visible on the x-rays."

"Seems like when there is an arm or shoulder injury, it's al-ways the right one," Kirby observed.

"In my case, that's a good thing," Judson told him. I'm a lefty. A few years back I was a southpaw relief pitcher for the Adairsville High School Tigers. I even played one year down at Athens. I hear you played a little ball yourself."

"A little," Kirby responded modestly.

By this time Mrs. Rittman and Sheila had caught up with them. "Kirby, I want you to meet my charming wife. This is Lacy. Lacy, this is Mr. James Gordan's nephew, Kirby, and the lovely young woman beside him is his sister, Riley."

"Charmed," Lacy remarked, holding out her hand palm down, bent at the wrist.

Kirby wasn't sure if he was supposed to kiss her hand or shake it. He gently sandwiched the hand between his and held it for a moment. "It's good to meet you, Mrs. Rittman. I see where Sheila gets her beauty."

"Oh, she's not my real mother. She's my third one. She and Daddy have been married for five, or has it been six years now?" Sheila quickly replied.

"But this one is definitely a keeper," Judson Rittman replied after clearing his throat and casting a glance of disapproval toward his daughter. "Speaking of beautiful ladies, I hear you went through quite an ordeal yesterday, young lady."

"Yes, it was a bit scary, but it turned out okay," Riley replied, wondering how Rittman knew about the turmoil of the previous day.

"Our boys sometimes do get there on time. I for one am glad this was one of those times," Rittman added. "You folks must be relieved that James's murderer has been captured. I know that's a load off your minds."

"I don't know that Uncle James's killer has been caught. Chief Nelson tells me it's still an open case," Kirby told him.

"Surely you realize that Freddy is the killer. That boy has been a menace for a long time and all the evidence points toward him," Judson replied.

"I don't know about that, but I'm sure Chief Nelson will get to the bottom of it soon," Kirby replied.

"I hope so, but I don't have the confidence in our boy chief that you have. I suspect after you've been around a while, you'll understand what I'm saying."

"I've been in police work for a while now, and I've seen no reason to doubt Nelson's drive or ability. Seems capable to me," Kirby responded.

"I hope you're right, but I've watched him long enough to have my doubts. I think he's chief only because his father was once our city policeman. Incidentally, I hope you weren't offended by my recent remarks about those people you're assisting. It's just that I love our little town. My family goes back four generations. I don't want to see a lot of riffraff come in and destroy our quality of life."

"I don't think our cleaning crew is going to hurt the quality of life here. The fact is, I think hardworking people like them will help us improve that quality. We were just talking this morning about the need to get those children into Sunday school." Kirby smiled at Rittman thinking, *I shouldn't be telling a fib right here in the church parking lot, but I sort of like getting his dander up.* He looked toward Riley, Amos, and then Carol to see they all had a puzzled look on their faces.

"Please don't bring those children to this church. We don't need to have them mingling with our children and grandchildren," Judson Rittman responded.

"Didn't Jesus say, 'forbid not the little children to come unto me,' or words to that effect?" Kirby asked.

"But not here. Send them to a church where they will be a better fit," Rittman pleaded.

"Maybe I should go where I'll be a better fit," Kirby countered.

"No, you need to stay right here in this church," Sheila quickly suggested. "We love having you here, don't we Daddy?"

"Why, of course we want you to attend our church. Wouldn't want it any other way." He smiled.

"You know that hardly anyone else in this church holds the kind of view you just heard from Judson, don't you?" Amos asked after they had reached their automobiles and were getting ready to get in.

"I know that," Kirby answered. "I understand there are a few people in just about every congregation with those kinds of prejudices, but usually they're not as vocal about it as Mr. Rittman."

"I hope you don't go to hell for lying, Kirby Gordan," Riley told him. "Nobody has said a thing about getting those children into Sunday school."

"I know, but perhaps we should've been talking about it," Kirby offered.

"I think you're absolutely right about that. I don't care what Judson Rittman thinks, I'm going to start working on those kids," Carol declared.

"Good for you," Amos responded. "You work on the children and I'll work on the parents."

****

"Beautiful," was the way Riley responded when Connie modeled her new black dress for her and Beth. "And it fits perfectly. No alterations needed with this one."

"I shouldn't have bought it. I couldn't really afford a new dress, but when I saw it and realized it was my size, all restraint was gone. I'll skimp somewhere else, but I had to have this dress."

"You made a good decision. It looks great on you," her mother told her.

Connie went back into her bedroom to change into her jeans and t-shirt. "I wish she could find a good job like she deserves so she can buy whatever she wants," Beth said. "It's been eight years since her dad passed and it hasn't been easy, but we've managed to get by."

"Does she have any good leads?" Riley asked.

"The best possibility is in Charlotte, North Carolina. It's the home office of a chain of banks. She wouldn't have to start at the bottom. They also told her the chance for advancement would probably come quickly. I think they're ready to hire her, but because of me, she's reluctant to take it."

"Would you go with her if she takes an out-of-town job?" Riley inquired.

"That's what she wants, but I couldn't do that. I've lived here all my life. All the family I have left is here. Those that are gone are buried here. It's all I know. I couldn't move to North Carolina, Tennessee, or even Dalton, Georgia. My home is here in Adairsville."

Connie returned to the room. "What's Mom been telling you?" she asked.

"Oh, we've just been talking about things in general," Riley answered. "I'm sure glad you ladies invited me over. I need an occasional reprieve from that gloomy brother of mine."

"He doesn't seem gloomy to me. Maybe a little arrogant, but not gloomy," Connie surmised. "I suspect he's a little bit of a playboy, a girl in every port, as they say."

"Are we talking about the same guy?" Riley asked. "We have to twist his arm to get him to say hello to any girl. He loved his wife as much as a man can love a woman. When she broke his heart, leaving him for his best friend, he just fell apart. He didn't seem to be interested in anyone else. She was his only love, going all the way back to childhood. His heart seemed to hang on to her when his mind knew there was no chance for any future for them. I'm certainly sad that her life ended as it did, but I'm hoping Kirby can now get on with his. I'm pulling for him to find the right girl with whom he can spend the rest of his life."

"I hear you've been in church a couple of times since you've been in town. You make me a little ashamed of myself. We used to attend church occasionally when Dad was still living, but Mom and I have gotten out of the habit in these last few years."

"Why don't you go with us next Sunday? I'll come by, and we can all three go in my car and sit together. It would give you an opportunity to wear that new dress," Riley added.

"Does Kirby also go to church?" Connie shyly inquired.

"He went with us this morning. It felt so good having him next to me in worship again after all these years."

"So, Kirby had gotten away from the church?" Connie asked.

"After Sherrie left him, and then Mom and Dad's sudden deaths, and, I guess, his losing the opportunity to play baseball, he has had to work through some things. But I think he's getting there. And you know what else I think? I think he likes you a whole lot."

Connie visibly blushed. "Well, I hope so. I want everyone to like me. I'll plan to go to church with you next Sunday. Maybe I'll be able to talk Mom into going with us." She was attempting to pull the conversation away from a discussion about Kirby liking her.

"We'll see," Beth responded. "I don't know if I have anything to wear. I don't have a new dress, you know."

"Here we go, Mom. You have plenty of clothes you could wear to church. But if you aren't comfortable with them, we'll buy you something new before next Sunday."

The ladies had a delightful Sunday afternoon of getting to know one another. Before Riley left, they enjoyed Beth's special taco salad. It was at the table that the first mention was made of the recent troubles. "Have there been any other attempts to break into your house?" Riley asked.

"Nothing," Connie responded. "We've seen nothing else of the would-be thief, regardless of who he was."

"At least not in his capacity as a burglar. We may see him every day, not knowing he was the one wearing the mask or the person taking that shot at us," Beth stated.

"Don't say that, Mom. I'd hate to think he's one of our friends or neighbors."

"But she's right, you know. It could be anyone. Best to stay on guard," Riley warned.

When Riley rose to go home, Connie asked her to wait a second before hurrying to another room to return with a folder. "Give this to Kirby. It's the work I promised him."

On her way home, Riley had a smile on her face when she acknowledged to herself, *I think I've found that special friend I've been praying for here in Adairsville. Carol is great and I've already learned to love her like a mother, but I need someone my own age. And just maybe she'll become Kirby's best friend too.*

CHAPTER 16

Before nine o'clock Monday morning, Riley delivered the folder Connie asked her to give to Kirby. Five minutes later, he was at his dining room table with the contents spread in front of him. *She certainly does comprehensive work*, Kirby concluded. There was no doubt in his mind that Earl Lance was Edwin Langley, the long-time fugitive it seemed the authorities had forgotten. Several facts convinced him that Lance and Langley were one and the same. First there were the duplicate initials, E.L. It was not unusual for someone choosing a new identity to use the first letter of the previous name. He had seen that happen twice before in his short time as a police officer. Back in the day, Langley's girlfriend, the one suspected of being his accomplice in the escape, was named Barbara. Lance's longtime wife was also Barbara. No doubt they were the same person.

The information in the files revealed another interesting detail tying the two identities together. Earl Lance had spent most of his life working with animals in some capacity. Coming out of high school, Edwin Langley had ambition to be a veterinarian. When the unfortunate fatal drunk-driving incident occurred, he was working as a farmhand to earn money that would enable him to start his college work. Kirby felt sad, almost sorry, for the fugitive. Not knowing the whole story, he saw it as another life destroyed by alcohol. How many times had he seen it before: a promising youth's ambition halted by the careless use of strong drink?

So, is Earl Lance Uncle James's murderer? Is he the person who broke into the study and the Reece home? Did he take a shot at one of the Reece ladies? It all fit. If he knew Uncle James had discovered him to be a fugitive, he had a motive. The break-ins possibly were efforts to recover the printed records of his identity. He may have tried to eliminate Connie because she learned his secret by doing the research. Kirby doubted a stronger motive for the crimes could be found. Surely, he was the one, but still. . . .

Kirby pondered those questions for a while, examining and reexamining the material he had in hand. He glanced at the time visible on his microwave to see that it was just five minutes until he was to meet Amos for a trip to the North Georgia mountains. Amos planned to introduce him to their hardware stores and lumber business in Ellijay and Blue Ridge. Kirby was looking forward to seeing that part of the state for the first time. Amos also spoke highly of the barbeque found in the region. The plan was to test it for himself at lunch time. It occurred to him that he was going to have to curtail his time with Amos or he would soon be fighting a weight problem. Amos seemed to be the kind of guy who could eat as often and as much as he desired and never gain a pound. Kirby, on the other hand, believed he could gain five pounds by simply smelling certain foods.

They were soon on their way. "Which will be the first stop?" Kirby asked.

"That would be Ellijay. We should be there in about an hour," Amos told him. "Ellijay is a nice little town that not so many years ago was occupied mostly by natives of the area. Now, you will find many weekend people from the Atlanta region as well as a good number of tourists. The permanent population is also growing significantly. The real estate business is a major industry. Houses are being constructed regularly. It's a good location for a hardware and lumber business. Blue Ridge isn't much different. These two stores have historically been among the most profitable of the bunch."

"This is beautiful country. Hard to believe we're only a little over an hour out of Atlanta," Kirby remarked.

"It's my favorite place in all the world, I guess," Amos responded. "We'll soon be to Pickens County. That's where my family lived for several generations before we moved to Adairsville when I was in middle school."

"That surprises me. I thought your family had deep roots in our town."

"We do, but we've only lived there for a little over fifty years. Both my father and my grandfather were firmly established in one of Pickens County's leading industries back in the day. They were moonshiners. Grandpa Edwards enlisted in the army at age sixteen to fight in World War I. He served in Europe. I guess it was the first time he'd been out of these hills, but that didn't keep him from doing his duty. He came home a highly decorated nineteen-year-old. The problem was that there was, at the time, little work to be found in this isolated area. The old community barber, getting along in years taught him the trade. But Grandpa soon discovered that, even when the elderly barber passed, there still wasn't enough work to support his family. It seems the boys up here in those days didn't bother with haircuts very often. Many of them received cuts from their mothers or wives rather than paying the quarter required to go to the barber.

"By then Grandpa had taken a bride and was the father of two small children. He needed to find a sideline. The bootleg liquor business seemed to offer the best opportunity. Grandpa Edwards was soon running a still full-time and cutting hair part-time."

"And I suppose your father just took up the family business as he became an adult?"

"Yeah, only it was before he was an adult. He was helping Grandpa run the still by the time he was twelve years old. Later, when making the stuff became too risky, he went into sales. He delivered liquor for some of the others who were willing to risk producing it. There were still some dry counties around the state in those days, and that's usually where Dad delivered. He was also known to peddle some of the liquid corn to locals right out of our old garage. Two dollars a pint, as I remember. He bought it by the gallon, so he made a pretty good profit."

"What changed? How did your family end up in Adairsville?" Kirby asked as they rounded a curve.

"Look at that, isn't that a beautiful sight?" Amos pointed to a large pasture covered with bright green grass with more than a hundred cattle grazing. "It doesn't take much to impress me. A green pasture with a herd of well-fed cattle will do it every time. How we got to Adairsville is simple. Daddy decided he wasn't being fair to his five children by raising them in that kind of environment. So, he got a job in a textile mill in Calhoun for little more than minimum wage. It was cheaper to rent a house in Adairsville than Calhoun, so we moved to Adairsville."

"And from that time on, everything fell into place I assume," Kirby speculated.

"Not exactly. Even though Grandpa made moonshine all those years, he was never much to drink. That was not the case with Dad. It was always around. From the time he was in his middle teens, he started using it. After we moved to Adairsville, he tried many times to quit, but could never quite get a handle on it. It never hindered him from working forty or more hours every week, but it did cause a lot of other problems that have haunted me, my brothers, and sisters to this day."

Kirby came to a stop sign at a major intersection. "Which way here, Amos?"

"You need to take a left."

"So, I assume your high school years were not an easy time," Kirby guessed.

"You could say that. It wasn't easy at home, but I had lots of good friends my own age. That was helpful to me and sometimes enabled me to shut out the problem at home. Mom died when I was a junior in high school. The next year and a half were a struggle for me and my brothers and sisters. As soon as I finished high school, I enlisted in the army. I figured I might as well go ahead and get it over with rather than waiting to be drafted. Almost right out of basic training I was sent to Vietnam. It was the most terrible thing I've ever been through, but there was a positive side. I found a family there among my comrades. I got to know some of the best men I've ever known during my two years in the jungle. Look over there!" Amos sudden interrupted his story to point left. "Isn't that one of the most scenic views in the state of Georgia?"

"It's magnificent all right," Kirby had to agree as he glanced to the west, able to see the beautiful foliage for miles. Not a house in sight. The shadows produced by a bright sun in the blue sky greatly enhanced the scene. "Tell me what happened after Vietnam. I want to hear all the Amos Edwards story."

"Unlike several of my close companions, I came out of the fighting there physically unscathed. But it taught me the horrors of war. I had several close calls, but I wasn't hurt, at least not physically. The worst part of it for me is that I'm sure I personally took the lives of several people. I've never been able to get over that. After all these years, it still keeps me awake some nights. I was fortunate to spend most of the last two years of my enlistment in Texas. While there, I met a lovely young woman. We fell head over heels in love, as they say. We were married six months before my discharge. Life was wonderful, and together, we made big plans. But it was not to be. A month before I got out, she was killed in a terrible car accident. I lost it. I guess you could say I went off the deep end. I remained in Texas for a couple of years and fell into a rather wild lifestyle. I'm not proud of it, but I tried just about every vice a young man could find in those days: drink, drugs, women, the whole ball of wax."

"It's hard for me to imagine you like that. You're probably one of the most together men I've ever known."

"There was a time when I was just the opposite."

"When did Carol come into the picture? It seemed to me from the first moment I knew the two of you, that you were made for each other. I never dreamed you were married before."

"While still in Texas, I sunk to the bottom. It was then that, by chance or perhaps by providence, that an older gentleman by the name of Tate Cummings, a devout Christian, became my friend. He took me under his wing and the rest, as they say, is history. I got back on solid ground, came back home, and got reacquainted with Carol. After we were married, I spent a little time in the technical school over in Rome learning about business, book-keeping, and finances. Life was good again, perhaps even better than the five months I spent with my first wife—a time of happiness I thought could never be duplicated. From there, my life has gotten better and better with each passing day."

"Wow, you amaze me, Amos. I guess I thought you came out of high school the guy you are now, found Carol, and settled down as a productive citizen in your hometown. Life hasn't always been easy for you either."

"I don't know if life is easy for anyone. Oh, our struggles differ, but we all have them," Amos suggested.

Suddenly the traffic up ahead slowed to almost a standstill. Kirby was able to see that the slowdown was caused by a tractor pulling a piece of farm equipment. After three or four minutes of creeping along at turtle speed, the driver of the tractor pulled over to let the cars pass.

Kirby remained silent, reflecting for a few moments before speaking again. "I guess I had just about everything I wanted or needed shortly after high school. I loved sports and getting to play pro-ball was a childhood dream come true. I couldn't remember when I didn't love Sherrie. I thought we would soon be living in a major league city together, growing more and more in love. I had the most supportive parents in the world. In a short period of time, I lost it all. I then started believing that happiness was impossible for me. Some of my friends down in Florida and from my high school and college days talk about how lucky I am to inherit Uncle James's estate. But I want to tell you, Amos: I would give it all to regain what I once had. I'm beginning to think I've spent the last few years of my life feeling sorry for myself when I should have understood I'm not really an exception. It's just that I've had to go through a set of problems different than those of the next fellow. I'm in your debt, Amos, for sharing your story with me. You'll never know how much it's encouraged me to know what you've gone through to become the person you are. For the first time in a while, I'm starting to get a little excited, about the future, wondering what's in store for me down the road."

"It's called *hope*, son. Don't you ever let go of it. There are few attributes more important to us than hope. Without it, life can be pretty sour."

"You've given me a lot to chew on, Amos. I guess I need to work on digesting it. You and Carol have taken us under your wings as if we were your own, and I want you to know we appreciate it. I want to shift gears and ask you one more question. What can you tell me about Connie Reece? How do you feel about her?"

"You starting to get a little crush on her, are you, son?"

"Well, I don't know about that, but I do find her fascinating. She's different, more independent than most of the girls I've known."

"She's had to be independent since her dad died. Her mother is a fine lady, but she's not the take-charge type. That's probably the fault of her husband, who, incidentally, was one of the finest men I've had the privilege to know. He pampered her, did everything for her. When he died, she was totally unprepared for life without him. The boy isn't a lot of help. He just wants to do his own thing. So, Connie stepped in and took charge. She's a strong girl. Her social life, most certainly, has suffered because of her devotion to her mother. Otherwise, I suspect she would have already been snatched up by one of our outstanding young men, or maybe on her way up in some marvelously successful company somewhere. I would love to see her in a situation where she can bloom into the flower she deserves to be. Your Uncle James noticed her. He spoke often of her potential. I think he had ideas about helping her along."

"Since he never got around to completing that task, maybe we can do it for him. Perhaps we can open some doors for her," Kirby suggested.

"You got something in mind?" Amos asked.

"No, nothing in particular. Not yet, but I'm thinking about it. I have an idea she would resent our interference should she know about it, so I think we had better keep our ideas to ourselves. I wouldn't want to offend her."

"No, we don't want to do that." Amos looked carefully at the face of his driver. That face took on a slightly different look, a glow, when speaking of the girl. *I believe he's falling for her. That couldn't be bad, could it?* he asked himself. "You'll want to turn left when you come to the next intersection," he instructed Kirby. "Let me tell you a little about Rollie Williams before we arrive. Rollie has been in the hardware business all his life. He's been at this store for almost thirty years, which was several years before James owned it. He will retire in two or three years. He's the person you need to spend some serious time with if you want to learn the business. He not only knows hardware and retail in general, but he's a capable teacher as well. On two occasions we've sent new managers from our other stores here for a month so Rollie could educate them. Each time it paid off."

Kirby was surprised at the size of the store when he pulled into the parking area on the south side of the building. He was especially impressed by the amount of lumber he saw in a large shed attached to the back of the main building.

"Lumber is a big part of our business here. We own our own portable sawmill which we use to provide much of the wood we sell here. If you want to learn about hard work, I suggest you spend a day with our guys at the mill," Amos told him. "I did that once about three years ago. I've not had an urge to repeat that performance since."

"You said the mill is portable. So, how do we get the timber? We don't own land here, do we?"

"No, we don't. Randy, our sawmill foreman, finds good acreage and negotiates for timber rights. There is no shortage of forest in these mountains. Getting people to let go of the timber is the hard part. Usually we come out better than if we buy the lumber from a wholesaler, and at the same time we keep several men working. Well, let's get out and take a gander. The barbeque is waiting. I hope you will not hesitate to ask all the questions on your mind."

Kirby did ask enough questions to keep them there well past Amos's anticipated barbeque, feast time, but that made it that much better when they did get to it.

CHAPTER 17

On Tuesday morning, Kirby left before nine o'clock to keep an appointment with their attorney in Cartersville. Riley and Carol left shortly afterward to handle some chores that would not take them out of town but would keep them away from home for at least a couple of hours. Amos was the only person home. He was at his computer doing some essential work on the James Gordan foundation's books.

Because people often came to the front door that opened into the apartment on the main floor, James had rigged that doorbell to be heard upstairs. Amos, knowing Kirby was not home, left his desk in response to the bell. He opened the door to see a man he did not at first recognize.

"Mr. Edwards, I don't know if you remember me, but I'm Earl Lance. We met once, and more recently, we had a close encounter. I would like to talk with you for a moment, if I may."

When Amos realized the man who most likely killed James stood in front of him, he became a little unnerved. He looked down to see if Lance held a weapon in his hand. He felt relieved when he saw none. "Yes, sir," he said. "I remember you." Hesitating to ask a possible murderer inside, Amos took a step toward the man and closed the door behind him. "I'd be happy to hear what you have to say."

"First, let me tell you I'm truly sorry for almost running you down in that pasture over in Plainville. I saw you coming, realized who you were, and I panicked. I jumped into my Jeep and took off. I didn't mean to hit you or even come close. It just happened."

"Why were you alarmed when you realized who I was?" Amos asked.

"I was sure you and Mr. Gordan had figured out my identity after I submitted that work application. I knew it was a mistake when I did it, but I needed a decent job to make ends meet, so I took a chance. I've managed to stay free all these years by being careful. I violated one of my first rules by putting all that information on paper. When Mr. Gordan began to ask me about my early life, I knew I was in trouble. I knew there was a good chance that a smart man like him would put it together."

"Then you are Edwin Langley?" Amos asked.

"Yes sir, I am. I'm not a bad guy, but I made a terrible mistake in my youth, and it has greatly troubled me ever since. Now I know I should have gone ahead and served the time for my crime. Had I done so, I could now be living my life, a free man, without the fear and guilt that has haunted me for almost all my adult life."

"Why are you here now, Lance? What do you intend to do now?" Amos asked.

"I'm on my way to your police chief to give myself up. I may have to spend the rest of my life in prison. I know there will be some time to do, and I'm not a young man. But hiding and walking on eggshells all the time, with a guilty conscience, has just gotten to be too much. My close call with you and your partner brought me to my senses. I'm ready to face the music."

Hearing the man talk, Amos had lost his fear of him. He didn't appear to be the monster he thought he was. "And what about Mr. Gordan's killing? Did you do that?" Amos asked.

"What? No, I didn't kill him. I heard it was an accident. I couldn't do anything like that." Lance's attitude immediately changed. "They aren't trying to pin that on me, are they? I'm not about to take the rap for something I had no part in."

"If you're in the clear, then I'm sure nobody's going to try to hang it on you," Amos told him.

"I don't know. I'm going to have to think about this. I don't mind being punished for a crime for which I'm guilty, but it's not fair for me to have to take the blame for someone else's wrong-doing. I'm going to have to think about this." The distressed escaped prisoner turned away from Amos and headed toward the Jeep Amos remembered from their earlier encounter. He got in the vehicle, started the engine and turned it to head toward the main road. Amos could barely make out the numbers and letters on the license plate, but he squinted and was able to keep what he saw in his mind until he got out the pen and notepad in his pocket to record the information.

Amos watched the Jeep turn right on Highway 140 to go east, away from town and the police station. He took his phone in hand and punched the appropriate button. "This is Amos Edwards. Could I speak with Charley Nelson?" After a moment, he spoke again. "Charley, I just had a visit from Earl Lance who admitted to being Edwin Langley. He said he was headed to your office to give himself up, but when he left here, he went in the opposite direction on 140. He could have gone north or south on the Interstate or stayed on 140 toward Pine Log. He's driving a Jeep with license plate GIF 387. He just left, so your guys might be able to catch him."

About twenty-five minutes later, Amos, who was still in the front yard, saw the police chief's car coming in his direction. Charley, getting out of the car, called out, "Well, apparently he got away. We had the guys in Calhoun waiting on him at the first ramp to the highway there. The same with the help of Cartersville going south. Me and my guys were hightailing it east on 140 with a state patrolman who happened to be in the area leaving from Pine Log coming this way. No one saw him. It would seem he had to take one of the country roads running off 140. We'll keep looking. He couldn't have disappeared into thin air."

Charley took about ten minutes to question his friend about Lance's visit. "I think I made my mistake in telling him he was a suspect in James's death. That seemed to be what spooked him," Amos told the chief. "If I hadn't let that out of the bag, he probably would've gone to your office and would be in custody by now."

"We don't know that he really intended to do that. It may have been some kind of trick he had up his sleeve. He would have to be a crafty dude to dodge the authorities all these years," Charley suggested.

"He sure seemed sincere to me," Amos responded. "I think when he arrived here, he genuinely intended to give himself up."

Amos was in all his glory, relating the incident to the others as they returned before noon.

****

Wanting to talk with her brother without being obvious, Riley suggested they go to dinner in Cartersville. "Someone recommended the Appalachian Grill," she told her brother. "I would like to give it a try."

"Okay, I'm game if you and Amos will let me fast for the next two or three days. Dining with the two of you is going to make me a blimp. Just because we can now afford to eat whatever we want, doesn't mean we should."

"We're not forcing you to eat anything you don't want to eat. Follow my example. Use a little restraint," Riley suggested. Also, it wouldn't be a bad thing for you to start running with me in the mornings."

"I think I might take you up on that. I do need to do a better job of staying in shape. Maybe I'll start tomorrow, if you promise not to make me look bad. I need to keep my image as a former professional athlete intact, you know."

Kirby insisted on taking the Highway 41 route rather than the interstate when they got ready for the short trip to Cartersville. "The interstate will be quicker," Riley argued to no avail.

"Only by about five minutes. The drive is more enjoyable the other way," Kirby responded.

Riley thought it strange that Kirby was more interested in the scenery than the time. That was contrary to his usual preference.

"A dinner theater production is being presented this weekend at the Adairsville Opera House above the 1902 Stock Exchange. Guess what? I've been invited to go," Riley told her brother, almost before they were out of the driveway.

"That's great. I know how much you love theater," Kirby responded. "Who invited you?"

"Mike Unger," she quickly answered.

"I don't think I've met him," Kirby replied.

"You know him. He's that cop that Amos is always kidding me about."

"Oh yeah. Amos must've been right. Are you sure you want to get mixed up with a cop? I know a little about guys in that line of work, and I have to tell you, if he's typical, I'm a little reluctant to see my sister get involved in such a relationship."

"I'm not getting involved in a relationship, I'm just going to a play with him. You're a policeman, and you're okay."

"Are you sure, sis?" Kirby laughed. "I'm just kidding you, honey. I'm sure he's a fine young man."

"There's just one thing." Riley's words were deliberate.

"I knew it! I can tell by the tone of your voice. There's something you want from me. I thought you were a little too anxious to spend the evening with me. What is it?" he asked.

"That's not fair. I love spending time with you."

"Yeah." Kirby said the word in such a way as to make Riley feel dishonest. "Go ahead. Tell me what it is."

"It's just that I don't know Mike. I wouldn't feel comfortable going out with him alone. I told him I would go with him if we could make it a double date. I asked him if you and a date could come along."

"And how did he take to that idea?" Kirby inquired. "Every guy I know would just love to go on a date with a girl and her brother."

"He doesn't mind. He said he just wanted to spend some time with me, and if that's the only way, he's willing."

"He must really think highly of you." Kirby laughed. "And where am I going to get this date? Have you arranged that as well?"

"I haven't arranged anything, but I have a suggestion. Why don't you ask Connie?"

"That's a good suggestion. I would love to spend some time with Connie, if she's willing. The problem is, I don't think she even likes me. I doubt she'll go with me."

"She just doesn't know you yet. This would be the perfect opportunity for the two of you to get acquainted."

"I tried that once. It didn't work out too well," he declared.

"Well, it'll be different this time. I'll make sure of that," Riley added.

"No matter how much you want it, you can't always make things work out your way. No matter what you say or do, she may not change her mind about me. For your sake though, I'll ask her. We'll see what happens. Incidentally, what's playing? Is it something worth watching?"

"According to Mike, it's *On Golden Pond*."

"That sounds good. Tomorrow I'll give Connie a call, and we'll see what happens."

After a couple of minutes of silence, Kirby pointed to the left. "There's where Pleasant Valley Road runs into Highway 41," he stated.

"Why is that important?" Riley asked.

"I don't know for sure that it is, but I've got an idea that Earl Lance or Edwin Langley, whichever name you prefer, is laying low somewhere near here."

"Why do you think that?" Riley asked.

"Because Pleasant Valley Road starts off as Mosteller Mill Road which intersects with Highway 140 three or four miles east of the 140/75 intersection. Then it becomes Pleasant Valley Road.

That very well could be where Lance got off 140 after leaving Amos. Connie put in the notes you delivered to me that Lance has or had a close friend who resides at a house on 41 near the Pleasant Valley/41 intersection. He could have made a right on Mosteller Mill Road and kept driving until he got to 41 and then to his friend's house."

"What makes you think he's hiding out with that friend?" Riley asked.

"I don't know that he is, but I think he might have unintentionally given us a hint to that possibility when he told Amos he was on his way to give himself up to Chief Nelson. Why would he give himself up to the Adairsville police if he wasn't staying near here? This isn't where he committed the original crime, nor did he escape here. Yes, Uncle James lived and was murdered near Adairsville, but according to Amos, Lance had no knowledge of being suspected of that crime until Amos informed him. It was when Amos revealed it, that he panicked and took off. If he was still living in Rome or one of the other towns in the area, he probably would've given himself up there. I think he was ready to surrender to the Adairsville police because it is the closest to where he is now staying. It's just a theory, but I think it's worth investigating. I plan to go by Chief Nelson's office first thing in the morning to talk with him about it. Maybe we can have Lance back behind bars before the day ends tomorrow."

"So that's why you wanted to take this route to dinner. You wanted to survey the area where you think your fugitive is hiding," Riley accused.

"It doesn't hurt to know the lay of the land," Kirby suggested. "I thought I might even spot that Jeep he drives, but no such luck so far."

Riley said little to her brother until they got to the restaurant. Once there, Riley ordered pecan chicken smothered with cherry sauce. Despite several uncommon dishes on the menu that tempted him, Kirby went with his old standby, the ribeye steak.

While waiting for their food to be served, Riley tried to think of a way to casually introduce the subject she really wanted to discuss with her brother. She believed he was pulling it together after Sherrie's death and the lingering troubles from before, but she wasn't sure. Maybe he was hurting as much, or even more than before, while putting on a good front for her sake. Unable to come up with a smooth transition to the subject, she finally just blurted it out. Afterall, this was her brother. "Kirby, I need to know how you're doing. You know, with Sherrie's passing and the whole mess before. If you would talk with me, I wouldn't have to be so blunt. Are you holding up? Is there anything I can do to help you?"

"Thank you for asking, sis. The truth is, I'm hanging in there. I'm trying harder to get on with my life than I have any time since the split. For a while, I just didn't care. It was, get up each day and try to survive."

"I know, and that's what worried me." Riley smiled at her brother. "It seems to me you're doing better, but I wasn't sure. Sometimes you're hard to read. It will help if you'd occasionally talk to me."

"I'll try to do better in the future," he told her. "I won't lie to you. I still struggle at times. Recently, when Amos and I were in Blue Ridge, we went by a beautiful lake. Since Amos was napping, and I needed a little noise, I had the car radio on. A beautiful instrumental version of 'Unchained Melody' came on the radio. You might remember that was Sherrie's and my song. Suddenly, I was back in upstate New York, sitting propped against a tree beside a lake. Sherrie was asleep with her head in my lap. I remember thinking, *this is perfect. It doesn't get any better than this, and we have the rest of our lives for moments like this.* Turns out, we didn't."

Then Kirby's voice broke, and he was silent. Riley could see he was unsuccessfully fighting back tears, and she now felt pain of her own due to her big brother's hurt. She reached across the table to cover one of his hands with her own. "I understand," she said. "You don't have to tell me, I understand."

Shortly thereafter, the waitress brought their meals. Brother and sister talked of things they had not talked about in years. They spent a lot of time recalling their parents and the wonderful life their mom and dad had given them in their younger years. When they left the restaurant, Riley felt closer to her brother than ever before. She was glad she had insisted he take her to the Appalachian Grill on Church Street in downtown Cartersville. They were family again. It was an evening she would not soon forget.

CHAPTER 18

Kirby explained to Chief Nelson why he thought Earl Lance—or more correctly, the escapee, Edwin Langley—could be found at the home of a man named Daniel Roper on Highway 41, north of the Cass area.

Listening closely to the logical presentation of his visitor, Charley immediately decided he might have something. "That makes sense," Charley told Kirby. "I'll look into it." The chief remained at his desk after Kirby left the room. He decided he liked the well-heeled detective from Florida. *He's a good investigator with instincts he's not afraid to act on. He doesn't stay in one place very long. He doesn't use a lot of unnecessary words. I could use a man like that on my own force, but I guess the forty thousand I could offer him wouldn't be enough to snag a man of his means.* Charley knew the first thing he needed to do was to get the address of this Daniel Roper. Within five minutes, without even leaving his desk, he had it. *Computers are wonderful instruments.*

Charley called in two of his officers. "I want you to drive down to this address," Nelson told them, handing one of the men a piece of notepaper. "Stay out of the sight of anyone who might be in the house. See if there's a Jeep there with Georgia license plate number GIF 387. If so, immediately radio me. If it's not there, try to find a place where you can inconspicuously observe the house. Let me know if the Jeep shows up."

Twenty minutes later, Charley heard from his two officers. "We're watching the house, but there is no Jeep or any other vehicles here."

"Stay out of sight and keep watching. Maybe it'll show up soon," he told them.

Charley opened the folder labeled "Edwin Langley." The file had only been created in the last few days. It wasn't until he became a suspect in the James Gordan murder that Charley had even become aware of the man and his successful disappearing act. He was amazed that a young man, still in his teens, could escape, vanish, and stay completely out of sight, evidently near the place of escape, until almost the age of eligibility for social security. How was it possible? Scanning the files, he saw although law enforcement never seemed close to recapturing Langley, they aggressively worked the case for at least five years. But then, they sort of forgot him.

The five years of aggression was easy to understand. Nobody likes to lose a prisoner. It's the worst thing that can happen to a department. Naturally, they would work, day and night, to set it right. He would be severely chastised by most law enforcement people for saying so, but Charley thought maybe the let-up in the search came because the man was not a hardened criminal, but a boy with promise who made a couple of bad mistakes. Apparently, all the years he had been on the run, he had stayed out of trouble, which was one of the explanations for his success. Often fugitives are caught because they can't stay clean. So why would he have killed Mr. Gordan? It didn't make a lot of sense. *I suppose there are people who will do just about anything to maintain their freedom. Langley's initial escape might be an indication he is one of those people. The murder of James Gordan might be further evidence.*

****

"Hello Kirby. I don't know if you remember me. I'm Al Jensen. We recently met at the Little Rock," the pleasant voice on the phone stated.

"Yes, I remember. You're the banker," Kirby responded. "What can I do for you?"

"I hope you don't mind. I got your number from Amos. I needed to tell you that your uncle had a safety deposit box here at the bank. Since no one has inquired about it, I thought it might have somehow been overlooked. Come by with the key if you want to take a look. If you can't locate the key, come on by anyway. Since you're the administrator of your uncle's estate, we can take steps to get you into the box. I was surprised Amos had no knowledge of it."

"Yeah, there's not much he didn't know about Uncle James's business. He had my uncle's complete trust. Thank you for the information, Mr. Jensen. I too was unaware of such a box. I'll get by sometime soon."

Kirby strolled from his living room to the study. Before flipping the light switch, he admired the Good Shepherd stained-glass window in all its beauty. As always, the lights were on behind it. It occurred to him that just a few days earlier, seeing the window stirred emotions completely different than those he felt viewing it now. Looking at the window in the days after first arriving in Adairsville usually produced resentment, despair, hopelessness, sadness, and maybe a little guilt. His impulse was to turn away from it. Now, it seemed he couldn't keep his eyes off it, and it lifted his spirits to see it.

Kirby seated himself in the chair behind the desk and opened the long middle desk drawer. He immediately saw three keys in a small tray. One of the keys was large and had numbers etched onto it. He put it into the right pocket of his jeans. Sitting at the desk with his phone now lying six inches from his hand, he decided, *I might as well go ahead and do it. This is Wednesday and the event is Friday. I'm late already. If I know her, she'll be offended by that.* He snatched up his phone and called Connie Reece's number.

"Hello Connie, this is Kirby Gordan. I hope you're having a wonderful day." He felt sweat starting to pop out above his brows.

"So far it's been good," Connie replied.

But I'm about to complicate it, he thought. "I'll get right to the point," he told her. "There's a play, I think it's On *Golden Pond,* being performed this Friday night at the dinner theater. Mike Unger is taking Riley. If you're willing, I'd like for you to go with me."

"Sounds like a fun evening. I love your sister. Mike has been a friend for a long time. I'd love to go," Connie declared.

"You would?" Kirby asked, sounding excited, but totally surprised. "That's great. I'll have Riley call you with the time and any other details. I'm looking forward to sharing the evening with you."

****

Six Adairsville policemen, including Chief Nelson, were part of the group of ten law enforcement officers approaching the Daniel Roper home from different angles. The remaining four officers that made up the posse were Bartow County Sheriff's deputies. Charley rang the doorbell and waited for a response. At first none came. He saw the curtains move slightly in the window to his right. That tipped him that someone on the inside knew the police were on the front porch. He rang again. After a long minute the door opened. A short man in jeans and a t-shirt, perhaps five-eight, who looked harmless enough, stood in the doorway. Charley had been involved in enough of these situations to know people weren't always as harmless as they looked, and conditions weren't always as safe as they appeared. He was ready for whatever would occur.

"I'm Charley Nelson, the Adairsville Police Chief. I'm looking for Earl Lance."

"Come on in, chief. This is Earl Lance." Three of his officers followed him into the front room. The other six remained outside in positions that allowed them to surround the house. The man pointed toward another sitting on the sofa.

"Mr. Lance, I'm going to have to ask you to come with me. Would you hold out your hands please?"

Lance stood and held his hands together out in front of his body. One of the officers placed cuffs on his wrist. Mike, would you read him his rights?" As that chore was being handled, a medium sized long-haired dog began jumping on Lance's left leg. The canine wanted Lance to lift him.

"Can I reach down and calm Jack?" he asked. "I think he's a little upset that I'm being carried away. He's been a member of the family for almost twelve years."

"Sure, go ahead and pet your dog," Charley told him.

"It'll be all right, Jack. Daniel will take care of you until Barbara gets here," Lance said while rubbing his handcuffed hands across the dog's head and back. Daniel Roper, the man who earlier came to the door, moved over to lift the dog and hold him with his head over his shoulder.

Lance was placed in the back seat of one of the county patrol cars. Charley took one of his officers along with him to Cartersville. He sent the others back to Adairsville. He wanted to be there for the booking and immediate interrogation. Charley felt relieved that a fugitive had been recaptured, but he couldn't help feeling a little sadness for the man who, regardless of whether he murdered Mr. Gordan, was probably going to lose his freedom for the remainder of his life. If not all of it, at least most of it. Sure, it was his doing, but that didn't take away the sorrowfulness of it all. Justice wasn't always pretty.

****

"I've got to tell you: I was part of the interrogation, and I have serious doubts about Lance being your uncle's murderer. It wasn't just that he denied doing it. I expected that. Few people readily confess to murder even when their guilt is undeniable," Charley told Kirby, who showed up at the police department almost before he arrived on Thursday morning. Kirby knew Lance had been arrested the previous day. He wanted to know if the fugitive revealed anything about Uncle James's killing. "My gut tells me he's not a killer," Charley continued. "I've been wrong before, and I may be wrong this time, but I don't think he's the kind of man who can plan and pull off a murder. Whoever killed Mr. Gordan planned his actions. He knew exactly what he was doing."

"I've never met Lance, but I agree with you," Kirby revealed.

"Why?" Charley asked. "How can you rule him out without interviewing him?"

"I haven't completely ruled him out, but a series of seemingly minor factors appear to eliminate him. For instance, you may remember the boys camping nearby said the guy who seemed to be the principle killer used the phrase 'our boys' in reference to our police department. That would seem to imply he was local. Now, I know you arrested Lance near here, but that wasn't his home. He was, at the time of the murder, living in Rome and had lived there for some time. He in no way could be described as a local citizen who might refer to your police force as 'our boys.' I know that's not conclusive, but there's more. The man who shot at the Reece ladies and later broke into their garage was clearly lefthanded. I think we must conclude it was the same person who killed Uncle James, attempting to keep Connie from telling something he thought she had learned through her work. Connie told us the shooter in the park aimed his rifle from the left side and later picked it up with his left hand after dealing with the dog. Mrs. Reece said the man running from the garage carried his rifle in his left hand. I'm told Lance is righthanded. Then there is the way the attacker treated Beth's dog. Lance is an animal lover who would not likely stoop to such brutality."

"I suppose it's possible the Reece ladies' problems were totally unconnected to Mr. Gordan's murder," Charley replied, playing devil's advocate. "Maybe a righthanded man killed him, and a lefthanded guy who doesn't like dogs was the culprit in the Reece incidents."

"That's possible, but both of us know it's not likely. The chances of two people so closely connected being the targets of violence at nearly the same time is a little much to be totally unrelated."

"There is one more fact that points away from Lance," Kirby added. "What kind of vehicle was he driving when you arrested him?"

"It was a Jeep," Charley revealed. "The same vehicle he was driving when he came by your place to talk with Amos and the same one he was driving when he almost ran you and Amos down in that pasture."

"Yes, and the records Connie gave me showed it's the only vehicle he's owned over the past three years. Barbara, his wife, has driven the same old green Ford for the past six years. The boys beside the road said the car they saw was a big, dark late model car. I found the same thing when I questioned a neighbor after the garage break-in at the Reece home. I think you arrested an escaped convict yesterday, but I believe Uncle James's murderer is still at large."

"Do you have any ideas about who that murderer could be?" Charley asked.

"No, none I would want to discuss now. I don't want to point a figure at someone based on a couple of obscure observations, but you will be the first to know if I discover anything concrete."

Kirby went by the bank after leaving the chief's office. He needed to get the contents of the safety deposit box of which Al Jensen spoke earlier. Before leaving home, he had gone into the study for one of Uncle James's old briefcases. He now carried it with him into the bank. He recalled a case in St. Petersburg where a robber carried such a case into the bank and handed the clerk a note, telling her to fill it with loot. He hoped he and his briefcase didn't trigger any alarms.

"Could I have a moment with Mr. Jensen?" he asked the clerk.

"Just a minute," she replied, studying the briefcase. "May I ask your name?"

"I'm Kirby Gordan," he told the clerk.

"Oh, I'm glad to meet you, Mr. Gordan." She no longer appeared concerned about the briefcase. "Miss Adams, would you go see if Mr. Jensen is available? Tell him Kirby Gordan is here to see him," she requested of a young woman behind a desk, who got up to walk across the lobby into an office located between two others. In a moment, she returned with Al Jensen. She too glanced at the case in Kirby's hand. Evidently the Gordan name didn't mean anything to her.

"Mr. Jensen," Kirby said, moving the case from his right to left hand and then holding his right out to greet the man approaching him. "I'm here to collect the contents of that safety deposit box you told me about."

"I'd be delighted to help you, Kirby. Did you find the key?" he asked.

"Maybe," Kirby pulled the large key out of his right pocket. "Could this be it?" He held the key in the palm of his hand for Jensen to see.

"That's it," he told Kirby after checking the number, "Let me go get our key. It requires both to open those boxes, you know."

In a couple of minutes, he was back. Kirby followed him to the back and handed Jensen his key, allowing him to release the box which he handed to Kirby. "You can use the desk in here," he said indicating a small room with a desk and chair. Just replace the box and remove your key when you are finished." Kirby opened the box and took a couple of minutes to examine the contents. He saw no thousand-dollar bills. In fact, there was no cash at all. He saw only papers and letters. He took all the contents out of the box and put them into the briefcase. Returning the box to its proper spot, he went through the door to find Mr. Jensen waiting for him.

"Thank you, sir," he said to the banker.

"Glad to help," he told Kirby, then continued to talk. "Mr. Wakefield, one of our long-time board members, recently passed away, leaving us a vacancy. I wondered if you would mind my submitting your name to our board chairman as a possible replacement?"

"I appreciate your confidence in me, Al, but I haven't yet made up my mind if I will live permanently in this area. You wouldn't want a nonresident serving on your board. I might recommend Amos Edwards. He handles our finances superbly. He would be an asset to you or any other institution," Kirby suggested.

"Amos Edwards." Jensen said the name as if it were new to him. "Amos, I would never have thought of him. That's worth thinking about."

The power of money, Kirby though walking through the parking lot toward his car. *Mr. Jensen knows nothing about me as a person, but because I inherited a lot of money, he's ready to add me to his board. Amos is, perhaps, the most capable man with money I've ever known. He's been around here for years and everyone knows him and the kind of man he is. But Jensen has never thought of him. Having a lot of money, it seems, somehow makes one more capable. We apparently live in a world easily blinded by the almighty dollar.*

After Kirby arrived home and parked his car in his customary place, he looked for Amos. He found him along with Carol and Riley in the couple's apartment. Carol was knitting. Riley was in a chair with Max in her lap. He wasn't sure what Amos had been doing before he broke into the peaceful scene. "Amos, there are some letters and papers in this briefcase that I got out of Uncle James's safety deposit box at the bank. I'm going to leave them with you to see if there is anything important there. I figured you would know more about that than I. There's no hurry. Whenever you can get to them will be fine."

"I'd be happy to look at them. I hear you've got a date with our girl, Connie," Amos said with some obvious delight.

"So that's what you three were doing before I came in. You were sitting around evaluating my social life. It didn't take you very long, did it?"

CHAPTER 19

Kirby tried to stay busy throughout the day on Friday to keep his mind off his plans for the evening. It wasn't that he was so excited about attending a dinner theater production. He had seen plays on Broadway. This was just an amateur production with a good dinner tacked on. His eagerness about the evening came from his yearning to win over Connie Reece. He felt as if he had gotten off to a bad start with her. He would have his work cut out for him to turn things around. Would having Mike and Riley with them be helpful or put him at a disadvantage? He wasn't sure.

During the early afternoon, Kirby heard a knock on the door of the study where he sat at the desk with papers from the business files spread out. "Come in," he called out.

"Sorry to bother you," Amos said after opening the door. "But there're two concerns I need to bounce off you."

"No problem," Kirby responded. "I needed a break from all these figures anyway. I don't know how you people who work with this sort of thing do it day after day."

"You've got to love it, or it will bore you to tears. It just so happens I have an aptitude for it. I can spend hours at a time with nothing but spreadsheets and reports in front of me and enjoy every minute of it," Amos told him.

"More power to you. I can make myself do it for a short time if necessary, but I never enjoy it. It's a chore for me to balance my checkbook."

"That's something you and your Uncle James had in common. Personally, I'm glad he felt that way, otherwise I would've missed a lot of good years with him. I hope to give you another two or three years, but the time will come when I will retire. Have you given any thought to what you'll do then?"

"Some. I've pondered it, and I do have an idea. Could you use an assistant to work with you until the time you decide to retire?"

"Sure. We could keep a full-time assistant busy, and still leave plenty for me to do, especially if you decide to return to Florida to live. James was so hands-on with the hardware stores and lumber business that it would be hard to get the same results without another capable overseer. I suppose you're thinking that person would be learning the ropes to take over when I retire," Amos added.

"That's exactly what I have in mind. Do you think we can justify it financially?" Kirby asked.

"I believe in the long run such an addition will make you money. And even if it doesn't, it's not going to break you, son. The bottom line is that you'll have someone equipped to take over when I step aside."

"I can't say I'm looking forward to that time. I worry about how I will manage without your counsel. Riley says she's willing to help all she can, but at the present, she's most committed to getting that law degree. That is as it should be. I figure the law degree will someday be a definite advantage to the Gordan enterprises."

"Do you have anyone in mind?" Amos asked.

"I do, but I think I'll keep that to myself for now. When the time comes, I'll talk with you and Riley before taking any action. The three of us will need to agree before anyone's hired."

"Can I conclude you're thinking about the same person I would recommend to you?' Amos asked.

"Well, as I said a moment ago, I'm going to keep it to myself right now, but I've got an idea that we're on the same page. Now tell me. What were those two important matters you came down here to talk with me about?"

"I almost forgot about those. The first is that I got a call from Rayford Barnes. You remember him? The bookman from Alabama. He wants to know if you'd be willing to sell the book collection if he should upgrade his offer."

"I haven't discussed it with Riley, but I think I would like to keep the collection, at least for now. If I was going to practically give it away as Barnes wants me to do, I would make sure Davis Morgan got it for his shop. If I'm going to donate it to someone, I think I would want the more respectable bookman to have it. However, I may want to talk further with Mr. Barnes about Uncle James's murder. It would be good if you could make sure you have a way of reaching him at all times."

"And the second matter is the big one," Amos told his young employee. "I want you to look at this. It was among the papers James had in his safety deposit box. I almost missed it. It was tucked away in an envelope labeled 'family notes.'" He handed Kirby two sheets of paper.

Kirby took a few minutes to look over the document. "It looks like a certified personal note. Uncle James loaned this person $150,000 with a plot of five acres as collateral. The note was due more than a month ago."

"Those five acres have frontage on Highway 140, near the highway about a quarter of a mile from here. It's prime commercial property, worth a lot of money. Did you notice the name and signature on the note?"

"Oh, yeah, I see it." Kirby continued to look silently at the paper in his hand. "Let's keep this between you and me for right now," Kirby instructed when he finally spoke. "This may have more significance than the money involved."

****

Riley returned mid-afternoon from the beauty salon located on the Central Block in downtown Adairsville. She had not seen a stylist since arriving in Adairsville. With her date coming up tonight, she thought it would be a good time to correct that. She liked the way her hair turned out, and she thoroughly enjoyed visiting with Wilma, the lady who worked the magic. Riley was looking forward to the evening. She wanted to get to know Mike Unger. He seemed like the kind of companion who could keep an evening enjoyable, but, at this point, she wasn't interested in a steady boyfriend. She was focused on a law degree; however, she did feel the need for some fun and relaxation. It should be a nice evening, especially with them doubling with Kirby and Connie. This would be a first. She had never double-dated with her brother before.

Now she had to decide what to wear. She knew Connie would wear her new black dress, so she needed to stay away from anything black. She selected from her closet a navy-blue dress that was one of her favorites, not overly dressy, but not too casual either.

She was glad Kirby suggested they purchase tickets for The Cleaning Crew and their wives. Amos and Carol planned to serve as their babysitters. They would also allow the crew to use their vehicle to drive to the event with the stipulation that Juan not drive. She looked forward to seeing the ladies in their new dresses. She wanted it to be a special evening for all involved, but especially for these ladies who had clearly missed so much of life.

At about six o'clock Riley heard Amos and Carol leave. Ten minutes later Kirby got into his car and drove away, no doubt on his way to pick up Connie. It was about five minutes later that Mike arrived in his shiny red Mazda, looking handsome in gray trousers, a blue button-down open collar, and blue blazer. He had a big smile plastered across his face when Riley got to the door. "I'm hopelessly in love" were his first words upon seeing her.

"You'd better hold those kinds of statements until you get to know me," Riley said, laughing. "You might discover I'm a real witch."

"What you are is an angel, a living angel from heaven," Mike responded.

****

Kirby and Connie were among the first ten people to arrive at the 1902 Stock Exchange. Ten minutes later the number had more than doubled. He didn't know any of the people who were there except banker Al Jensen. He recognized several faces he'd seen at church. Bill and Judy, Jessie and Alice, along with Juan and Louise, were among the next wave of people to arrive. Kirby was proud of The Cleaning Crew. Likely, no one there had any idea that less than a month earlier, they were homeless, living in tents behind a cemetery, and getting food out of dumpsters. He and Connie walked over to where they stood looking perhaps a little ill at ease. Connie smiled and remarked to the ladies about how pretty they were.

"I can't believe Amos let you use his car. He doesn't let anyone besides himself behind that wheel. I figured he would make you drive that old work van," Kirby laughed. The whole group appeared to immediately loosen up. Kirby wanted them to enjoy themselves.

"He did demand that we keep Juan out from under the wheel," Bill laughed.

"Driving lessons not going too well?" Kirby asked.

"Let's just say, you don't want to be on the road when he's operating a vehicle." Jessie looked Juan's way and smiled.

When Riley and Mike arrived, Kirby waved at them. The couple hurried to join them. Kirby could see delight on the face of the young policeman, no doubt put there by virtue of escorting the most beautiful lady in the place. And Kirby didn't doubt for a moment she was the most beautiful. Only one other came close. She was his date. That black dress did something wonderful for

Connie. He had been attracted to her from the beginning, but until now he hadn't realized how truly pretty she was.

Kirby panicked when he saw who walked in behind Mike and Riley. It was a smiling Judson Rittman with his wife Lacy on his arm. He wouldn't put it past Rittman to raise a ruckus over the presence of The Cleaning Crew and their wives. The man had no tolerance for people he saw as different, and he didn't mind telling the world about it. An irrational outburst would be the sure way to kill the evening and bring down his friends who were making so much progress. Kirby kept a close watch on Rittman from across the room in the minutes before the dinner bell rang. Even though he saw him glance in the direction of the three couples, his attention went back quickly to the person he was at the time, trying to impress with his importance. Kirby concluded the glance was a result of one couple being Hispanic and another African-American. Despite that, they didn't look too different than the remainder of the crowd, so Rittman evidently didn't recognize them. Kirby was relieved when the dinner bell rang, and they started upstairs without incident. It occurred to him that sparks surely would fly if the hostess had placed The Cleaning Crew at the same table as the Rittmans. He breathed a sign of relieve when he saw they were on opposite sides of the large room.

The food was excellent. Kirby doubted Mike noticed. He couldn't keep his eyes off Riley. *He'd better be careful if he wants any kind of relationship with Riley. All it takes to cause her to run like crazy is a little over-the-top attention.* "Tell us a little about yourself, Mike. Are you originally from Adairsville?"

"I grew up just up the road near Calhoun."

"How long you been on the police force?" Kirby asked.

"About eight months now. It doesn't pay a whole lot, but I enjoy the work," Mike replied.

"Tell me about it. Until I was promoted to detective, I was always having to cut corners just to pay the bills every month."

"You don't have to cut corners to pay the bills anymore, do you?" Connie broke in.

"No, I guess not. Thanks to a loving uncle who is no longer with us. One who had a propensity for business, But I would trade all the money to have him back," Kirby added. "He was the last member of my dad's family."

"I'm sorry about the way that sounded. It didn't come out exactly right. I intended no offence," Connie stated.

"I know you didn't. No offence taken."

The conversation was pleasant for the remainder of the meal, with laughter and other noise occasionally coming from their table. The best part of the dinner was the chocolate cake topped with raspberry syrup served for dessert with a cup of good coffee. The play was well done for small-town theater. Kirby was glad he had let Riley talk him into coming. He wasn't ready to end the evening when they walked down the stairs after the play concluded, but he could think of no way to extend it.

Kirby had almost forgotten about their friends on The Cleaning Crew. They were seated on the side near the stairs, enabling them to be among the first to exit. They were now out of sight. When Kirby and his group reached the street, walking toward where their car was parked, they met Bill coming toward them.

"Kirby, I locked the key in the car. Do you think you could go see if Mr. Amos has an extra one?" he asked.

"You don't need to do that. I can get you into your car." It was the voice of banker Al Jensen walking a few steps behind him.

"My husband can get past any lock ever made," a lady, Kirby assumed was Mrs. Jensen, stated.

"I was a locksmith in another life," Al told him. "I worked summers and part-time during college in a shop that dealt with nothing but locks. You don't find many of those today. Show me where your car is, young man, and we'll see what we can do."

Bill led the way. In less than three minutes, the car door was open. "And did you see that he managed to do it all with the wrong hand?" Mrs. Jensen said proudly.

"She won't let me forget I'm lefthanded," Al laughed. "The fact is, it doesn't matter which hand bankers favor. One can count money with either hand."

Kirby was driving Connie home when the phone in his pocket rang. He handed it to Connie. "Why don't you see who that is?"

"It says here it's Amos," Connie said, looking at the screen.

"Would you see what he wants?"

"Amos, this is Connie. Kirby's driving. I guess he has quirks about breaking the state law. Can I help you?"

"You'll do just as well. I've invited The Cleaning Crew and their families over for a little post-evening get together. Called Mike and Riley to invite them. They're on the way. Wanted to see if you two would join us."

Kirby heard the invitation since the phone was on speaker. "What do you think? Want to extend the evening a little?" he asked Connie.

"I would like that," Connie turned toward him with a grin and a pleasant look. "We'll be there shortly," she told Amos.

They talked, laughed, played with the children, drank soft drinks, and even ate some more. Kirby could recall no evening in recent years that he enjoyed as much. It all was good, but what made it perfect for him was he got to spend time with Connie. He sensed she was warming up to him. That made him extremely happy. It was well after midnight when he drove her home and parked in her driveway. Kirby got out to open the door for her.

"Kirby, I need to apologize to you. I formed an unfair opinion before I knew you. Tonight, I've realized you're just the opposite of the arrogant playboy I thought you were. I wouldn't blame you if you never spoke to me again. However, I hope you'll forgive me, and that we can be friends."

"You can be sure I'll forgive you. The opinions you formed were probably as much or more on me as on you. As to our being friends: yes, I want us to be friends, but I believe there is a chance that, in time, we can be a great deal more than that. I guess time will tell, but that's what I'm hoping for. May I give you a good-night kiss before you go inside?"

"I think I would be greatly disappointed if you didn't," she responded.

Kirby took her in his arms. Their lips met for about five seconds. Her lips were soft and warm producing a beautiful sensation he had not experienced for a while. It was nothing short of an incredible moment for Kirby. Yes, he could fall in love with this girl.

Beth Reece, carefully hidden in a window upstairs from which she could see all that was going on below, smiled and said quietly, "Hallelujah. She's human after all."

Kirby returned to his apartment in a state of bliss, but no sooner had he laid his head on his pillow did he begin to feel guilty. Would Sherrie always be there in the shadows?

CHAPTER 20

K irby was feeling moderately proud of himself on this Monday afternoon. He was returning from Dalton, where he had survived his first real business meeting without Amos. Maybe he could make the transition from policeman to business executive if he decided that's what he wanted. He saw Exit 306 ahead and instinctively turned the wheel in that direction.

When he passed the undeveloped property to his right, he saw three automobiles, all current models, parked there. Four men, two of them in suits and ties, stood on the lot. Knowing this was the parcel of land Uncle James had agreed to take as collateral on his $150,000, his curiosity was aroused. Since the note had not been paid on time, technically, that property belonged to the James Gordan estate.

Kirby took the road to the west that ran parallel to the plot boundaries. He made his way to the back of the lot where he found a spot in a grove of trees where his vehicle would not be seen. He got out of his car and hiked up a small hill to find a place from which he could observe unnoticed by the men below. From behind a growth of bushes, he studied the delegation. He recognized only one of the men. It was the friendly banker, Al Jensen. He had to wonder what this was all about. It no doubt was a business meeting of some kind. Reason would lead him to believe the meeting had to do with the property. Such conferences were not usually held on vacant lots so those involved could get some fresh air. He wished he could hear their conversation. After several minutes the group disbanded to get into their respective cars. Kirby waited until all had driven away before he reentered his own vehicle.

****

Riley was out back in the swing in Amos and Carol's garden, slowly moving back and forth with a low-sounding squeak coming from her seat each time it changed directions. Her mind was in recall mode. Her mother had always said she had the rare capacity to enjoy the good times over and over and the ability to immediately shut out the bad times. She was reliving the good.

"A penny for your thoughts." The voice from behind her belonged to a person who in recent days had become one of her favorite human beings. It was the voice of "the old man" himself, as Carol sometimes referred to him.

"I don't know that they are worth that." She turned her head to see a smiling Amos come up behind her to start pushing, causing her swing to travel a little higher. "I was just thinking about my summer thus far here in Adairsville. It's been fun, and a little adventurous. Even incidents like the Freddy Seals episode can make life interesting."

"Forget about Freddy, but tell me what you have enjoyed," Amos requested, as he continued to push the swing.

"Well, most of all, I've enjoyed getting to know and learning to love you and Carol. When I lost my parents four years ago, it left a huge void in my life. My mom and dad were special, and I know they can never be replaced. But you and Carol have come about as close as anyone could. I don't say that to flatter you. I say it because I mean it."

"I know you do. We feel the same way about you," Amos replied.

When there was a moment of silence, Riley turned to look into Amos's face to see that his eyes were starting to get red and puffy. He swallowed hard before speaking again. "I've always wanted to have a little girl to push in this swing. Maybe that's why I put it here. Carol and I once had a little girl who came to us late in life. We were already well into our forties, and our son had already departed in more ways than one. We were delighted to learn she was on the way. A short time before she was born, the doctor told us there were obviously problems. He advised that we abort her. He told us that decision would protect us from a lot of hurt and expense. Of course, we couldn't do that. We felt she was God's gift to us. When she was born, we were advised to put her in an institution. We never even considered such a move. The six months we were allowed to keep little Laura before she was taken home were among the most amazing months of our lives. So, we know what you're talking about when you talk about voids. You and Kirby fill a void for us as well."

"I'm sorry Amos. I didn't know. Carol has never spoken to me about Laura."

"Oh, she finds it extremely difficult to talk about her, but she feels the same as me. Every day we give thanks for our time with Laura. She taught us so much." Silence followed while Amos adjusted his suspenders before again speaking. "Tell me what else you've enjoyed in these last few weeks," he suggested, wanting to alter the conversation.

"There's been lots that has made me happy. All the quality time I've had with Kirby would be high on the list. I enjoyed last Friday night immensely. Mike was fun to be with, and Connie is rapidly becoming one of my best friends. I think I enjoyed the gathering at your place even more than the dinner and play. Making friends with The Cleaning Crew and their families has been a delight for me. I'm so pleased we've been able to help them get on their feet. Wasn't it great to have them in church with us yesterday?"

"It surely was. I can't read the guys and their wives very well, but I'm sure the children were thrilled with Sunday school," Amos told her. "If they have anything to say about it, they'll be coming back. I don't know how much they heard of what he said, but I hope Rittman's tantrum doesn't scare them away."

"He really is an unreasonable guy, isn't he? Did you hear what he said to Kirby? It sounded like a threat to me."

"Oh, the man doesn't mean half of what he says. He has some strange ideas and when those are challenged, he starts yelling. That's the kind of man he's always been. It takes all kinds, you know."

"I guess, but he scares me. I'm not sure his elevator goes all the way to the top," Riley stated.

Amos laughed. "That's a nice way of putting it, I guess. Don't let him get to you. He's a miserable man, and he wants everyone else to join him in his misery."

They heard a car pulling into the driveway. "That's probably Kirby," Riley speculated.

"Most likely. I felt bad sending him off to that meeting by himself. Those timber lease meetings can be bothersome sometimes. I could've gone, but I know he's trying to decide about whether to be a policeman or a businessman. I thought this would give him some hands-on experience that might help him make that decision."

"Which do you think he should choose?" Riley asked. "Which is he best suited for?"

"Naturally, I would like to see him remain here permanently, stepping into James's shoes, but I want him to be happy. He can do well with either task. He needs to choose whatever will make him happy."

"I suppose you're right. I've tried to stay away from influencing him, but it's hard. I love having him close by."

Kirby, hearing the voices in the back, came to join them.

"How'd the meeting go?" Amos asked.

"I think it turned out well. In the beginning, the owner had grand ideas about using us to get rich. He tended to be a little unreasonable. We got past that though. When I showed him the contracts we have with some other landowners in similar situations, he backed off. Then we were able to do business. Thank you for suggesting I take those along," Kirby said to Amos. "Incidentally, when I passed the property in question due to the note found in the safety deposit box, it looked like a meeting of some kind was going on out there. There were four men that I could see. The only one I recognized was Al Jensen. Do you know anything about that?"

"No. I've heard nothing, but it's something we need to investigate.

"Perhaps you could give Al a call and discreetly see what you can find out," Kirby suggested.

"I'd rather we continue to keep quiet for a while about why we have an interest in that property. However, if there're plans in the works for it, we need to know about them."

"I'll give it a shot. Most people consider me a nosy old coot and won't think twice about my inquiry."

****

The Cleaning Crew did most of their regular jobs in the evening when the businesses were closed to traffic. In addition to the Gordan apartments and rentals, they also worked two other apartment complexes, totaling over fifty units. It was their job to clean-up, paint, and do some minor maintenance before the new renters took up residence. They often did this work during the day. They were diligently involved with such an apartment on this Monday afternoon. Bill was doing some paint touch-up in a bathroom. Juan was working on the tile floor in the kitchen, while Jessie was running the vacuum over the living room floor. Suddenly, there was an explosion that all three men felt. It was a blast that could be heard even over the sound of the vacuum.

"What's that?" Bill shouted his question, running toward the living room.

Jessie was already at the window, pulling the curtains aside to look outside. "It's our van," he bellowed. "Our van is on fire. I told you we shouldn't let Juan drive."

"Juan didn't do that," Bill declared, now standing beside Jessie to observe the van being consumed by flames. Black smoke was rising above the now unrecognizable vehicle. He was immediately glad they had not parked it near any other vehicle in the lot, otherwise there could be cars exploding all over the parking lot. Bill pulled out the company phone he carried and called 911. Within minutes the firetrucks were on the scene, but all they could do was make sure the fire was confined. Meanwhile, Bill called Amos to report what had happened.

****

The pleasant gathering in the garden had just ended with Amos going inside to make his telephone call to the bank. Riley went looking for Carol to volunteer her help in making dinner to which she and Kirby had been invited. Kirby was in the study. Having just seated himself, he was taking his usual moment to admire the Good Shepherd window when he heard a knock and Amos's excited voice.

"Kirby, Kirby! The Cleaning Crew van has gone up in flames."

Immediately a dark feeling came over Kirby. "How are the guys? Did any of them survive?"

"Thank God, they're all okay. They were working inside when it happened. Nobody got hurt, but the van was totally destroyed."

"They were working inside, and the van was parked when it blew up? That doesn't sound right."

"That's how Bill reported it to me. Sounds like maybe it was sabotage."

"Where did it happen?" Kirby asked.

"Over at the Browning Arms Apartments."

"We'd better get over there," Kirby suggested.

"I'm going too," Riley, who had walked around the corner, told them. "Carol passed the news on to me. I want to make sure they're all okay."

Two firetrucks and several firemen were still there when they arrived at the Browning Arms Apartments. Several people, most residents of the complex, were standing around discussing the incident. Mike and another young policeman were walking among those asking questions.

Bill, Jessie, and Juan immediately hurried toward them when they got out of the car. "Mr. Amos, I promise you, we didn't do this. We had been inside working ever since we returned from our lunch break. We felt and heard the blast, then looked outside to see the van burning," Bill reported.

"We don't blame you. A van can be replaced. We're just glad you guys are all right," Amos told them.

Kirby shook the hand and patted the back of each. "It scared the living daylights out of me when I got the report. I thought one or more of you had been killed for sure," he told them.

Riley hugged each. She said nothing. She didn't have to. They knew how she felt.

Kirby walked over to where Mike was writing on a pad. "You must've found something. You're making notes," he said to his friend, thinking that a lighthearted approach might be the best way to get information.

"Not a lot," the relatively inexperienced Mike answered.

"Do you think it was a freak accident or did someone do this?" Kirby asked.

"If these guys are telling me the truth, and I've no reason to doubt them. I can think of no possible explanation as to why a van that has been sitting cold for almost three hours could suddenly explode."

"Did any of the residents see anything?" Kirby asked Mike.

"Two of them saw a middle-aged man they didn't recognize. Neither saw him in the immediate area of the van. They did say he looked suspicious and kept looking around as if he was afraid someone would spot him."

"Where they able to give you a description?" Kirby asked.

"Only that he was a middle-aged man, slightly graying, nicely dressed in a blue shirt. One of them thought he wore gray pants. The other said it was khakis. Maybe they were referring to two different people or one had a better memory than the other."

Amos arranged for a ride home for The Cleaning Crew. Before leaving, he told them he would try to have them back in business within a couple of days. "A van won't be hard to get. It's a good thing you had most of the equipment inside."

Mike and Riley talked for a couple of minutes before they got into the car for the ride home. "Well, I don't want to falsely accuse anyone, but I think we all know who was responsible for this fiasco," Kirby disgustingly remarked.

"You may be right, but let's not jump to any conclusions," Amos responded.

"All of us, plus numerous other people, heard him say in the parking lot of the church yesterday that he would make sure The Cleaning Crew would be out of business by the end of the week. And in case you've forgotten, he told us we would regret the day we crossed him," Kirby reminded them. "People like that don't need to be on the streets."

Knowing how upset Kirby was, Riley and Amos remained quiet for the five minutes it took for them to return home. Riley silently thanked the Lord that The Cleaning Crew had escaped unharmed.

"Incidentally, Amos, did you learn anything from Jensen about the deal out at the property?" Kirby inquired as they were walking to the front door after exiting the car.

"He told me there is a deal in the works to sell the land to a large gas station/truck stop chain. He said the company likes to involve local people in such deals and has secured the services of his bank to work with them on the finances. He seemed to think it was a big deal for our community."

"Maybe it is, but I think it's about time we approached him with the information we have. If it's valid, the deal needs to be called to a halt until some questions are answered. It will save everybody, including the purchasers, a lot of trouble."

At dinner that evening Kirby apologized to the others for his outburst earlier. "I know I've got to do a better job of controlling my temper," he told them. "The fact is, there're a lot of things I need to work on."

"You seem to be doing all right to me," Amos told him. "Sure, you've got some growing to do. So do I, and so does everyone else. That's always going to be true until we reach perfection. And perfection, I'm told, will only be attained when we get to heaven."

"Speaking of heaven, I'm planning to take Connie and her mom to see the Rome Braves play my old team from Lexington tomorrow evening."

"Are you comparing a baseball game to heaven?" Carol looked a little shocked.

"Oh, don't pay any attention to him, Carol. In his mind, heaven's going to be one never-ending, extra inning baseball game," Riley alleged.

"Hey, didn't you see *Field of Dreams*?"

"I thought it was a good movie, but I didn't exactly buy the theology," Riley laughingly responded to her brother.

"Regardless of what you think heaven is going to be like, why don't we make tomorrow evening a group outing? Why don't you three join us? Of course, all the players on the Lexington team when I was there are long gone. Some of them to the majors," Kirby said with a note of disappointment—or perhaps longing—in his voice. "The manager, however, is still the same guy. I could introduce you to him."

"Just like meeting Elvis," Riley teased him. "What do you think? You guys got anything to do? Sounds like fun to me."

"Let's do it. I haven't been to a baseball game in years," Amos stated.

"I don't know that I've ever been to one," Carol confessed. "Except when I used to watch my brothers and their friends play out in the cow pasture."

"It's still the same. The only difference is the cow pastures are now a little more elaborate," Riley declared.

CHAPTER 21

"When we get some wheels, we'll pay that piece of trash a visit," Bill told his two cohorts. "Mr. Amos and the Gordans have been good to us. I guess they had insurance to cover the loss of the van, but he needs to know he can't get away with that kind of stuff."

"But we don't know for sure it was him," Jessie reminded his friend.

"Oh, it was him all right. You heard the threats he made Sunday. And even if it wasn't him, he's the kind of scum that deserves a little roughing up," Bill remarked.

"I don't know about that," Juan spoke up. "Miss Riley won't like us punching anybody's lights out, no matter what they did. She would be sadly disappointed in us if we got into any trouble. What would our families do if we ended up behind bars? I think we'd better let Amos and Kirby handle it. We've got a good thing here, and we'd best not blow it."

"He's right. Do you remember what that preacher said in his sermon Sunday?" Jessie asked. "He said we should leave the revenge to God."

"I know he said that, but that's not what I was taught. When I was growing up, I was told to take up for myself. If you don't, no one else will," Bill responded.

"But we are learning that's not always true. Amos, Kirby, and Riley have been taking up for us," Juan reminded them. "Maybe we learned a lot of things that were not true. That may be why we were in such a mess when we came here."

"Okay, we'll chill. We don't want Riley losing faith in us, but we'll keep our eyes peeled for that fancy man who thinks he's running things around here. We'll be ready if he tries anything else. He needs to learn he can't hassle friends of The Cleaning Crew and get away with it."

****

"Amos and I have an appointment with Al Jensen at the bank late tomorrow. Maybe I need to see Rittman before then," Kirby told his sister.

"I don't know, Kirby. Maybe you ought to take Chief Nelson with you when you confront him. I know you're disturbed about what you assume he did to the Cleaning Crew van. Guilty or innocent, he's not going to receive any accusations well. He could be a dangerous man," Riley said.

"You forget, sis, that I'm a trained police officer equipped to handle such trouble."

"I understand, but sometimes precautions need to be taken regardless of how prepared we think we are. You're the only brother I have. I don't want to lose you."

"I'll take it under advisement." Kirby grinned at his sister. "Seems like those big pleading eyes are still allowing you to pretty much get your way, princess."

They ate a light lunch. "I'm saving plenty of room for at least two ballpark hot dogs tonight and we'll have to have peanuts. You can't go to a ball game without getting peanuts," Kirby declared.

"You're excited about going to the game tonight, aren't you?" Riley asked.

"Yes, surprisingly, I am. Can you believe this will be the first time I've been to a ballpark since I was cut? I've watched some games—or more correctly, parts of games—on TV, but I've not been able to drag myself to a ballpark. Even living in Florida with spring training going on all around me, the stadiums have not enticed me. I had some good friends in baseball, but regrettably, I've not stayed in contact with any of them. One of the reasons I'm so wound up about going to the game tonight is because Connie and her mother are real fans. It will please me to see them having fun."

"You're starting to fall for her, aren't you, Kirby?"

"I don't know sis, but I do know I'm more attracted to her than any girl I've known since Sherrie. Because of the way that turned out, maybe I'm overly cautious, but I like her a lot, and I want her to like me."

"I'm glad, because I think she's a special person. Don't let her get away," Riley cautioned.

"What about Mike? How do you feel about him?" Kirby inquired.

"I like Mike. He's one of the good guys. I hope we can continue to be good friends, but that's as far as it goes. I'm not romantically interested in him or anyone else until I get through law school."

"We'll see if you still feel that way when the right guy comes along in a year or so. I suggest you let Mike know how you feel. I think he's smitten. He's got something other than friendship in mind. I don't think you want him to be hurt."

"When did you get to be such an expert on relationships?" Riley asked, immediately regretting her careless words when she saw the hurt that came across Kirby's face.

"You're right. I'm the last guy who should be giving anyone advice about their love life." Kirby looked away from his sister.

"I didn't mean anything. I was just trying to be funny. I would trust your advice about romance or just about anything else. There's no one I respect more," she told Kirby while moving over to give him a brief hug. "Now tell me again about that note you found in Uncle James's things in the safety deposit box. I want to do a better job of helping you with business affairs."

Kirby spent the next few minutes explaining to Riley the implications of the note. "The bottom line," he told her, "is that if that note is valid, and it seems to be, then we own that property that is about to be sold for more than one million dollars."

Riley left her brother to run some errands. She hoped one careless statement didn't set back her brother's progress. He had been doing so well. *I wish I could kick myself, or better yet, learn to think before I open my mouth.* Again, she was reminded of how a few words, maybe no more than one short sentence, can so deeply hurt someone. She told herself she would be more conscious in the future of what she said when she opened her mouth to speak.

****

"I can't decide which outfit to wear," Connie told her mother when she came into her bedroom. Four outfits were spread out on Connie's bed.

"It's just a ball game," Beth reminded her. "You never gave much thought about what to wear to a ball game before."

"I know Mom, but I want to make a good impression tonight."

"Who are you trying to impress? Is it the manager, the umpire, maybe the fans in the stands? Just who is it?"

"Oh Mom, don't be so flippant. You know I want to impress Kirby."

"I thought you were having a hard time stomaching an arrogant playboy like him."

"What do you want, Mom? Do you want me to tell you I was wrong, and you were right? Well, I was wrong. When I got to know him, I learned he wasn't at all like I thought he was. You can save your sermon. I've learned my lesson about stereotyping people."

"You know I was just playing with you, honey. I couldn't be more delighted that you've found someone who meets your lofty standards."

"Here we go again," Connie moaned. "My expectations have never been *lofty*. It's just that I never wanted to settle for someone for whom I wasn't utterly fond."

"And you're definitely fond of Kirby!"

"Yes Mom. I'm fond of him. He's handsome and an extraordinarily strong person, but humble. He's kind and generous, and he knows how to make a girl feel like she's the only one in the world."

"Well, maybe we ought to stop the presses and report to them we've found the perfect man."

"I think he may be the perfect man for me. I don't know for sure, but I want to find out. I had just about decided to take that job in North Carolina, but now, I don't know."

"You realize he may soon return to Florida."

"He hasn't made up his mind. He may decide to stay here. Even if he does go back to Florida, he will be here as often as he can. His sister is going to make her home here, and he has businesses everywhere you look around here."

"You've got it bad, don't you child?" Beth put her arms around her daughter.

"Maybe I do. I'm not sure, but I know I've never felt about a man the way I feel about Kirby."

"God bless you, honey. It's the best feeling in the world and it's the most painful. I think that's how the good Lord designed love to be," she told her precious daughter. "Isn't it wonderful?"

****

Kirby followed Riley's advice and called Chief Nelson's office. "Nelson, this is Kirby Gordan. I've an appointment with Judson Rittman out at his place tomorrow at 2:30. I wanted to invite you to go along if you wish."

"What are you planning to talk with him about?"

"There're a couple of matters he and I need to chat about; starting with a discussion of the burning of a certain van."

"Before you go out there half-cocked, you need to know the evidence seems to clear him of any involvement in that crime."

"What evidence do you mean?" Kirby asked. "I heard there was a man fitting Rittman's description seen in the parking lot."

"That's true, but that man was never seen anywhere near the van. We had our guys go door to door to see if anyone we might have missed earlier saw anything that would be helpful to us. One of our officers talked with a lady who observed a young woman a few minutes before the explosion occurred. Not only did she see her near the van, but she saw her open the driver's door to put something in a bag inside. The lady who saw her said she looked to be in her twenties, and she was wearing a baseball cap with jeans and a white t-shirt. It appears Rittman had nothing to do with it."

"That's interesting. It's unusual for a woman to be involved with explosives. Considering the threats Rittman made on Sunday, I was convinced he was guilty," Kirby declared.

"I've known the man most of my life, and I know he's all mouth. You can take most of what he tells you with a grain of salt. I need to question your boys about any run-ins they might have had on the job, especially with any young ladies."

"You think someone might have blown up the van because the guys didn't get the toilet clean?" Kirby asked, amused.

"I've seen stranger things," Charley replied. "As you know, on this job, you don't dare rule out anything."

"I've a couple of other things I need to talk with Rittman about, so I'm going to see him anyway. You're welcome to come along if you want," Kirby told him.

"I'd take you up on that, but I'm leaving in a couple of hours. I'll be out of town for two days. I don't much like it, but these out-of-town meetings go with the chief's job. I'd be happy to send one of my men with you if you think that's advisable," Charley offered.

"No, I don't think so. I can handle it," Kirby responded.

"Well, let me encourage you to hold your temper. I guess you've already discovered Judson can be pretty annoying at times."

"Have you been talking with my sister about my temper?"

"Just offering a word of caution. I wouldn't want to have to lock you up," Charley chuckled.

After getting off the phone, Kirby continued to sit in his chair, pondering this situation that he thought he had all figured out. Now he wasn't sure. He would lay it all on the table when he met with Rittman tomorrow and see what happened. It could be interesting. But he didn't want to think about that now. He had a ball game to go to tonight with a lovely young lady. The last time he was so excited about going to a ball game, he was playing in a league championship.

****

Kirby had forgotten the energy that even a minor league ballpark can produce in the moments before the start of a game. "The Rome Braves are only a class A affiliate of the parent Atlanta Braves, but a lot of good baseball is played in ball parks like this one," Kirby remarked. "We are lucky to have them only about twenty-five minutes away from us."

"Almost every homegrown star on the Atlanta Braves team spent some time here in Rome. It's a great place to see the stars of the future," Connie pointed out. "Sometimes I think it's more fun to see them here while their talents are still unharnessed."

In the years since his forced separation from the game, Kirby had tried to keep baseball completely out of his mind. Being at the game tonight was something of a breakthrough for him. He saw Tom Patterson, the Lexington manager, come out of the dugout to stand next to the fence separating the fans and the diamond. He grabbed Connie's hand. "Come with me and I'll introduce you to a great baseball man." He guided her to the fence where Patterson stood watching his players take infield. "Tom Patterson, I thought you would have moved up a notch or two by now."

Patterson was silent for a few seconds while closely examining this man out of the stands. Then a wide smile came across his face. "Why, Kirby Gordan, the best catcher I ever had who couldn't hit a lick." He held his hand over the four-foot-high fence to greet his former player.

"I wasn't a three hundred hitter, but I wouldn't say I couldn't hit a lick," Kirby objected. "I usually made contact."

"Yeah, but the ball didn't go anywhere when you made contact. Who's this pretty little lady with you?" the manager asked. "Is this Mrs. Gordan?"

"I'm sorry, Connie. No, this is my friend, Connie Reece. Connie, this is my old manager, Tom Patterson, who once, a long time ago, pitched for the Boston Red Sox. As a manager, he seems to be stuck at class A."

"I know you won't believe me, Kirby, but I remain at class A because that's where I want to be. As I'm sure you remember, I'm more a teacher than a strategist. The best place for me is down here where I get to help these youngsters reach their potential. Tell me, Kirby, what are you doing these days? I lost track of you after you went to the University of Louisville."

"I've been on the police force down in St. Petersburg, Florida. They made me a detective a few months ago. I'm here presently settling my uncle's estate. He left me and my sister several businesses. I haven't decided if I'm going to stay and spend my time with those, or go back to Florida so I can continue to be a cop. I enjoy police work enough that I certainly would miss it. On the other hand, I've found a lot to like around here." Kirby turned and looked in Connie's direction.

"I see you have." Patterson grinned. "If you stay around here, come and see us often. Being in the same league with Rome, we're here several times a year. Connie, you keep this no-hit wonder out of trouble. He's one of the best people I've had the privilege of managing. Notice I said *people*, not player."

"I noticed you talking to that old guy. Who is he?" Amos asked when they returned to their seats.

"That's Tom Patterson, the Lexington manager," Connie excitedly said before Kirby could answer.

"So, he hasn't been lying to us. Kirby really was once a baseball player," Amos reacted.

"Yes, it seems he was a good field, no-hit catcher, but a great guy," Connie responded.

"That's not exactly true. I hit over two hundred one of the two years and I totaled twelve home runs. The primary job of a catcher is to take care of things behind the plate." Kirby was silent for a moment before continuing. "Who am I fooling?" he asked. "I was a good field no-hit catcher. That's why I'm currently a policeman and not a major league catcher making millions." He laughed.

Everyone but Riley had at least two hot dogs. She had one. Kirby wasn't sure, but he thought Amos might have eaten four. Several bags of peanuts were devoured by the group. The icing on the cake was that when the game ended in the tenth inning, the Braves came out on top, five to four. The evening was a success.

"There's something important I would like to talk with you about. Would you have breakfast with me at Cracker Barrel in the morning at eight?" Kirby asked Connie as they were returning to Adairsville.

"I would love to have breakfast with you in the morning," she responded moving a little closer to him on the car seat.

CHAPTER 22

The three-year-old sportscar stayed three cars back of Kirby's vehicle, close enough to follow him while not being noticed. When Kirby turned into the restaurant parking lot, the driver guided the sportscar to a location across the lot but was careful not to draw Kirby's attention. The driver closely watched him get out of his car to go inside but remained behind the wheel. *I can see everything I need to see from right here. Then I can take care of business.* The stalker looked at the pistol lying on the seat, picked it up, and turned it over to examine it closely. *This is one problem that will be eliminated today.*

****

It was 7:45 a.m. when Kirby arrived at the restaurant. Five minutes later Connie drove into the parking lot.

"You look fantastic this morning, but then I've never seen you when you weren't beautiful," Kirby said as she approached.

"My, my, you must have arranged this meeting to get something from me," she responded. "Nobody talks like that anymore unless they want something."

"As a matter of fact, this meeting is about exploring the possibility of obtaining your services, but my statement about your appearance has nothing to do with that. It's just fact."

"Someone told me you were shy. That didn't sound like the remark of a shy man."

"Some things just have to be said," Kirby replied with a broad smile.

After they were seated and placed their orders, Kirby jumped into the spiel he had been rehearsing in his mind for two days.

"Amos will retire in a couple of years. In the meantime, he needs an assistant to help him manage our businesses and investments. I've talked with both him and Riley. All three of us agree that you're the person we want for that job. We would like for you to come on board as assistant with the idea of taking over the top spot when Amos retires. We hope Amos will then continue as a consultant, but I think I can assure you he will readily turn the job over to you and stay out of your way. What do you think? Are you interested?" Looking at Connie, Kirby couldn't read her. Was she pleased with the offer or indifferent? Maybe even disappointed? He wasn't sure.

"There's one question I have before we go on with this," Connie responded after what seemed like five minutes to Kirby, but probably wasn't more than thirty seconds. "Are you asking me to take this position because you think I'm beautiful and you like me, or do you really believe I'm the person for the job?"

"Be assured I would offer you this job even if you were ugly and without any charm whatsoever. Your past work for Uncle James gave us a glimpse of your ability. Not that you are ugly and without charm," he added, suddenly aware of what he had just said.

"You'd better clarify that." Connie laughed.

"We don't know for sure, but we think Uncle James was just about ready to offer you a job when he was killed."

"He never said anything to me about that, but he did drop some hints from time to time, making me think that might be in his mind. I thought when he was gone, that opportunity went with him. I never dreamed I would be asked to run his affairs. I guess I need to ask you about the particulars of the job. Then there are such matters as salary and benefits."

"If you're interested, we'll set up a meeting with Amos. He'll talk with you about such matters. I can assure you that salary and full benefits will be generous. If they aren't generous enough for you, then they can be negotiated. One of the fringe benefits is that you'll be working closely with the owner," Kirby added with a grin.

"That'll be nice," Connie responded. "I do truly love being around Riley," she teased.

It was a good time for the waitress to show up with their breakfast. She placed their food in front of them. "Y'all enjoy your breakfast," she uttered as she walked away.

"I hardly know how to ask this question without appearing to be forward, but I do have one concern," Connie hesitantly said.

"Go ahead and be a little forward," Kirby suggested. "We want to get all the cards on the table."

"Okay, if you say so. What if I take the job and our relationship continues to grow? Sometime down the road we decide to uh . . . get married. Where would that leave us?" she asked.

"I want you to know that's not a forward question. It's one to which I've also given some consideration. The only answer I was able to come up with is that, should it happen, we'll work it out. There would be no problem should you want to continue the job. If you wanted to be a stay-at-home wife and uh . . . mother, that would also be good. Your preference would be the deciding factor."

"Then there's the other side of the question. Both of us know that sometimes relationships change. What if it doesn't work out for us, and one or both of us wants out? How does that affect the job?" Connie asked.

"It doesn't. We want to hire you because we're confident you can do the job. Our relationship, or lack thereof, has nothing to do with it. I don't want to think about us not being together, but whether we are or aren't doesn't alter your abilities."

"That's fair, if you really mean it."

"I do. Are you ready for me to get you and Amos together to discuss the details?"

"This is not a firm *yes*. I'm not saying I'll take the job, but I'm definitely interested, and will talk with him."

"Any particular time you prefer?" Kirby asked, sounding relieved.

"As soon as possible. I need a job soon," Connie declared.

They finished their breakfast, but continued, for some time, to sit at the table and sip coffee between exchanges.

"Enjoying your breakfast?" the vaguely familiar voice asked.

Kirby turned his head to see a smiling Al Jennings. "Hey Al. What's this? Did you lose your way? This is Cracker Barrel, not The Little Rock."

"Don't tell anyone," he said. "I wouldn't want them to think I'm unfaithful. It's just that I sometimes have to meet a client here."

"Incidentally, Al, I could be a little late getting to your office this afternoon. I have an appointment with Judson Rittman. I don't know how long that'll take, but I should be there in time for us to talk before closing time."

"No problem," he told Kirby. "Just get there when you can. I hope you and old Judson have a pleasant conversation. Just remember his bark is much worse than his bite. Did I tell you he and I were together down in Athens at the University of Georgia for one year? In fact, he and I worked together at that locksmith shop I told you about. The two of us just about ran the place for a while until he flunked out of the university."

"No, I didn't know about that. Tell me, is Judson as good around locks as you?" Kirby asked.

"I had a longer tenure there, but I suspect he could still do just about anything I can do, with locks that is."

Kirby was still on the porch shortly after Connie got into her car to drive away. Kirby was surprised to meet Amos and The Cleaning Crew headed for the front door of the restaurant.

"You guys are out early this morning," Kirby greeted them.

"Didn't I tell you last night? I guess I'm getting forgetful in my old age. The boys and I are going down to Cartersville to check out a van. If all goes well, one of the guys, not Juan, will drive it home."

"Great! Back in business. That's good news. Been talking with Connie about that position. Give her a call to set up an appointment to talk with her. She says the sooner, the better."

"Then she's ready to take the job?" Amos excitedly asked.

"She hasn't exactly said 'yes' yet, but I think she's on the verge. She needs to talk with you about the details we discussed. Didn't you eat breakfast before you left home?" Kirby asked.

"Just here for a morning snack, I suppose."

"The boys needed to get breakfast. Don't tell Carol you saw me here. She'll think I wasn't fond of that oatmeal she fed me."

****

After leaving Cracker Barrel, Connie noticed the car behind her continued to stay with her after each turn. She thought little of it. A neighbor on the way home, perhaps. She pulled into her garage to see that her mother's car was not in her spot. Then she remembered: Mom had a doctor's appointment this morning in Rome. There was a moment of guilt for not going with her. She knew her aging mom didn't always pay close attention to her doctor's words, making a second set of ears valuable. However, this one was a scheduled, routine visit. Mom should be okay without her.

Wow, Kirby had given her a lot to think about. She wasn't sure what she expected from the meeting, but she certainly had not foreseen being offered a job. To take the job would resolve her biggest problem right now, but she wasn't sure how she felt about it. She didn't want anything to get in the way of what seemed to be happening with her and Kirby. The job could do that. On the other hand, working together might draw them closer. If she took the job, she could even stay right here in Adairsville to keep an eye on her mother. But there were so many potential problems. Despite what Kirby said about job security in case of a break-up, she had doubts. Oh, she had no trouble believing he meant it, but . . .

Being deep in her thoughts, the ring of her doorbell almost startled her. She casually strolled over to the front door, turned the lock, and pulled open the door to see a familiar face, but one she had never expected to see at her door. The pistol in the hand of her visitor, however, was totally new to her.

****

Carol heard the ring of the phone she left in the kitchen. She hurried to the counter where she had laid it when she washed the dishes.

"Hello, this is Carol. Can I help you?"

"Yes, Carol. I'm sorry to bother you. This is Beth Reece. I'm trying to find Connie. I know she had breakfast with Kirby. I thought she might be around there. She and I are due in a few minutes to talk with the man at city hall about some problems we're having with our water meter. I wanted to make sure she hasn't forgotten. It's a little strange that her car is here in the garage, but she's nowhere in sight."

"Maybe she dropped the car off there while she and Kirby took his car somewhere," Carol suggested.

"That occurred to me, but she usually calls, leaves me a note, or something to let me know where she is."

"Well, you know how it is when you've found a new love. Sometimes, among other things, it causes you to be rather forgetful," Carol suggested with a giggle.

"It's been too long for me to remember how love affects one," Beth responded with a nervous laugh.

"If anyone else but me were home, I'd check to see if they know anything about her, but right now, I'm it. The rest are scattered around the countryside."

When Carol went outside to tend to her gardening a few minutes later, she decided she would call Amos to advise him of Beth's call. *She's a grown woman, a college graduate, a twenty-four-year-old who's perfectly capable of taking care of herself. I guess she can go anywhere she wants with whomever she desires. But . . .*

Carol took her phone from her apron pocket and punched Amos's number. No answer. *Amos is probably driving with his phone in his pocket, unable to answer due to Georgia law*, she decided. *He'll pull over to return the call as soon as he finds a place to do so.* No more than three minutes passed before her phone rang and she saw that it was her husband. She smiled, proud of herself for knowing him so well. "This is Amos. What do you need, honey?"

"It's probably nothing, sweetheart, but I'm a little concerned. Beth Reece called looking for Connie. Her car is in the garage at home, but she's nowhere to be found."

"I saw Kirby at Cracker Barrel. She had already left. He said nothing about planning to go anywhere with her. But if they had such plans, there was no reason to inform me. He may very well have left there and gone by her house to retrieve her."

"And why were you at Cracker Barrel?" his wife demanded.

"Oh, the boys had not yet eaten breakfast. So, we stopped to get them fed."

"And I guess you just had to have those biscuits and gravy to keep them from feeling bad about you watching them eat?"

"I'm sorry honey. The phone is breaking up. I've got to go."

"I'm going to break up his head," the annoyed wife declared under her breath before placing the phone back into her apron pocket.

****

Having eaten such a big breakfast at Cracker Barrel, Kirby decided after a trip to their Calhoun hardware store to skip lunch. If he did that, coupled with spending almost an hour on his recently purchased exercise bike, maybe he could make, at least, a tiny dent in that six pounds he had gained since being in Georgia. He seemed to become more aware of those six pounds every time he was around Connie.

Having a little time before he had to meet Rittman, he again drove up Boyd Mountain to look at the spot where Uncle James had been pushed off the road and down the hill. He got out of his car and spent more than thirty minutes at the site. He found nothing new. *It probably doesn't matter,* he decided. *I think I've got it tied down. Maybe we'll know if I'm right before this day is over.*

Kirby hoped he had his directions right. Rittman lived out on the old family estate located on Trimble Hollow Road where three or four generations of Rittmans had resided. It seemed that getting to that road was made difficult, first, when it was cut off by the highway, and even more so later due to a twenty-year-old industrial development. Kirby drove out of Adairsville going north on Highway 41. He turned right and, after less than a mile, veered again to the right. He soon saw what he assumed to be the Rittman Estate, a well-cared for older clapboard white house with a large front porch and several outbuildings scattered around the property. There was a good-sized barn nestled down the hill behind the house. Cattle were grazing in the pasture south of the barn. Kirby pulled into the driveway and took a deep breath. He got out and immediately felt the heat. *It must be closing in on a hundred degrees. Southern weather may be more pleasant in the winter, but I'll take the north during the summer.* Kirby had never been able to explain it, but there are times when it feels like something out of the ordinary is in the air. He had that feeling now and it was a little spooky.

****

Connie's captor first tied her hands together behind her back and then her feet. The rope was now tight enough to break the skin in some places. She was gagged with what appeared to be a dirty rag; then pushed hard to the floor. Her right shoulder was hurting due to the impact of the tumble. She wanted to cry, but she would not give her captor the satisfaction. She looked around the shed to see that farm equipment was stored in the building.

"I haven't decided what I'm going to do with you, sweetie. Maybe I'm attach some weights on your body and drop you in one of the ponds. I may decide to bury you. Perhaps I'll bury you alive. How would you like that? If you are a good girl, and lie here quietly, maybe I'll put you out of your misery with my gun. Don't you think that would be better than drowning or being buried alive?" With those threatening words, Connie's captor left the building, gun in hand.

Connie managed to turn her head about to see as much as she could of the contents in the building. She was determined not to die this way. She should still have most of her life ahead of her. What would her mother do without her? This couldn't be the end. Not now that she had found so many good reasons to live. Maybe she could find something with a sharp edge to which she could back up and cut the ropes around her hands. Her eyes continue to search.

She spotted an old-fashioned plow among the items on the end of the building farthest away from her. Perhaps the blade was sharp enough to cut the rope if she could get to it. On her stomach, she began to slither and using her toes against the floor to push while she slowly moved in the direction of the plow. When she reached her destination, she was able to flip her body over on her side to get her bound wrists in contact with the blade. She moved her hands up and down, working to cut the rope. It wasn't going to happen quickly, but she persisted.

It paid off. After a while she felt the rope give. She had succeeded in cutting through her restraints. Connie pulled her hands apart. The rope fell to the floor. She turned to sit while she reached down to release her feet. Soon she was completely free. She ran to the door of the shed to discover it was locked with a padlock on the outside.

There were two windows in the front wall. Connie tried both, but neither was designed to raise. She found an old dining room chair with the seat missing. She dragged it over to one of the windows and looked through the glass to make sure no one was close enough to hear. Using the chair, she smashed the window as quietly as she could. She picked the remaining glass out of the window frame, cutting her right hand in the process. She then used the chair as a ladder to get up into the window from where she dropped to the ground.

When Connie picked herself up from the grass beneath the window, her first impulse was to run as far as she could get away from the house. Then she observed something that brought her to a complete standstill. There was a car in the drive beside the house. She was sure the car was the one Kirby drove. *Maybe Kirby is in trouble*. She headed toward the house where she quietly pulled herself up on the porch. She stood beside one of the windows so as not to be seen by anyone who might be looking her way. She peeped inside.

CHAPTER 23

"Lacy is in Kentucky visiting with her mother. It's anyone's guess where Sheila is. So, I'm here all alone and can't offer you anything, but maybe a glass of water. Come on in and find a chair that suits you," Judson Rittman invited.

Kirby came through the big hallway to follow Judson into the sitting room where all the antique furniture was a perfect fit. "I wouldn't care for anything," Kirby told his host before being seated in a wingback chair with his back to the entrance. "There are some issues we need to talk about, Judson. I thought it best we do not wait any longer."

"If you're referring to what happened to your Cleaning Crew van, I want to assure you I had nothing to do with that."

"I have to admit that in view of the remarks you made Sunday, I felt you were the guilty party, but Chief Nelson assured me the evidence clears you of that particular crime; though I'm not convinced you had absolutely nothing to do with it," Kirby added.

"I'm telling you that I'm completely innocent! I didn't do it, and I didn't order anyone to do so!"

"I'm going to take your word for that, but that's not the major reason for my visit today. I'm here to talk with you about the note you signed with Uncle James, using the property you're about to sell for collateral."

"Yes, we did have an agreement like that. James and I worked together on several business deals."

"But according to the note I saw that property should have reverted to Uncle James's estate several weeks ago unless I missed something. You've never repaid the $150,000 you borrowed nor the interest."

"James and I talked about that before he died. He was willing to wait for his money until I sold the property. Funds are a little tight, but the sale solves that problem. You'll get your money soon as the transaction is completed."

"I'm not concerned about the money. I have to wonder if the desire to hang on to that property so you could complete your big deal, could be the reason for Uncle James's death," Kirby said with almost no emotion.

"Are you accusing me of killing James? James was my friend for more than thirty years. I could never harm him!" Rittman snapped.

"You have to admit that a million-dollar paycheck is a pretty good motive."

"But I told you that James and I worked that out."

"I've seen nothing on paper confirming that," Kirby countered.

"James and I were friends. We didn't have to put our agreements on paper."

"Evidently, someone thought it important the initial agreement be drafted. I have that document in my possession," Kirby replied.

"That was different," Judson argued.

"I fail to see why it was important to draw up a contract one time, but not another. The fact is, I was beginning to suspect you even before I discovered this motive."

"What possibly could have made you suspect me?"

"There were several red flags. None of them seem like much when separated from the others, but when grouped, they are rather compelling. For example, the two boys witnessing Uncle James being put in that car to be shoved down the hill, heard one of the men refer to the police force as 'our boys.' I heard you use that same phrase in reference to our Adairsville force on the Sunday morning when you were speaking to us about Riley's rescue from Freddy Seals."

"That doesn't prove anything. A lot of people use that phrase," Judson objected.

"You're right. That alone means nothing, but there's more. There is the description of the car at the scene on Boyd Mountain the night Uncle James was killed, as well as the one driven to the Reece home on the night of the break-in. Both descriptions fit your car perfectly. Then according to Connie, the man who shot at them in the park was a lefthanded shooter. Beth observed the man who broke into her garage carried his rifle in his left hand as he made his escape. I learned the day you had your arm in a sling, that you are lefthanded."

"I could name any number of men around Adairsville who are lefthanded," Rittman, now disturbed, pointed out.

"When Freddy was arrested, you appeared to be absolutely certain he was the man who killed Uncle James. Later you showed the same certainty about Earl Lance. Seems to me that you wanted someone—anyone—to take the fall before you started looking guilty. There's more. I learned recently that you once worked as a locksmith. We knew that, since there was no damage, the break-in of Uncle James's study and probably the Reece's garage required either a key or someone who knew about locks. You add all that to a motive like the personal overdue or soon-to-be overdue loan you could not pay, knowing it would keep you from finalizing the biggest deal of your life, and it looks bad for you."

"I can see how all of that makes me look guilty, but again, I promise you on my mother's grave that I didn't kill him."

"Chief Nelson will be back in town tomorrow. You'd better get your Ps and Qs lined up. As soon as he returns, I'm dropping all this on him." Judson did not respond to Kirby's warning, but rather quickly raised his head to look past Kirby. He had a startled expression on his face. Kirby turned to see what was drawing his attention.

"No Sheila!" Judson yelled as he jumped to his feet and took a step forward. It only took a moment for Kirby to see the source of Rittman's sudden outburst. Sheila Rittman was standing not more than eight feet away with a pistol in her hand.

"He's reporting no one to the police. A dead man can't do that," she declared in a voice strangely different than her normal speech. She sounded and looked like a totally different person. "He won't ruin my life or yours."

"Sheila, you can't do this again! We'll find a way to work it out. This isn't the way to solve anything. Put down that gun," the rattled father demanded.

"Listen to your dad," Kirby said, trying to make eye contact with the girl, but it was almost as if she didn't see him. "You don't want to do something for which you'll be sorry later. Give me your gun." He held his right hand out toward her.

"I'll not give you anything, you unscrupulous Casanova. We could have had a good life together. We could have gone places and done things. How could you choose that worthless Reece witch over me? Why couldn't you see that I could offer you so much more than she ever dreamed of having? We are two of a kind. She's nothing. But you can forget about her. She's out of the picture now. And you are about to go down."

"No Sheila!" Rittman again shouted when she pointed the gun directly at Kirby, intending to end his life then and there.

Kirby's mind told him there must be a way out of this, but in the split second he had, the only thing he knew to do was to rush her. He took his first step, expecting to hear the gun at any moment. But before the out-of-control girl could pull the trigger, something totally unexpected happened. A woman appeared from nowhere. From behind, she tackled the unsuspecting Sheila. As Sheila fell forward, the gun went off. Kirby felt the slug enter his right thigh. He went down as the wounded leg could no longer support him. He was now on his right knee with his left leg extended forward. The severity of Connie's blow had caused Sheila's gun to fall on the hardwood floor in front of her. She, now on her knees, was desperately scrambling to reach the pistol. Connie diligently hung on to the screaming madwoman for dear life. Sheila could get no traction. Kirby limped to the gun to scoop it up.

"Where did you come from?" Kirby asked in a voice filled with amazement. He was now holding his bleeding right thigh with his right hand. The gun was in his left hand.

"Is that all you can say?" Connie, now out of breath, asked. "I don't think I heard a, 'thank you for throwing your bones to the floor to save my life.'" She was now standing beside Kirby, allowing him to lean on her as he made his way to one of the chairs.

"Thank you, sweet lady. I was never so glad to see a person in all my life. Where did you learn to tackle like that?"

"Haven't I told you about my football experience? I was a tiger cheerleader. You can learn a lot from the sidelines," Connie declared with a grin.

Judson Rittman was on the floor helping his daughter to her feet. Kirby, using the gun in his left hand, motioned for the two of them to be seated on the sofa in front of him. Both were uncharacteristically silent. Sheila had a distant and unemotional expression when her father brushed her hair from her face and embraced her. The once arrogant pair were utterly subdued. Despite all that had happened, Kirby almost felt sorry for them.

"Better call 911 to get the police here," Kirby said, handing his phone to Connie.

Connie called for the police as well as an ambulance to transport Kirby. "Isn't it amazing how the most terrible events in our lives can turn out for good? Sheila bringing me here at gunpoint to tie me up in a shed out back was one of my worst experiences ever. But that dreadful indignity enabled me to be where I needed to be at exactly the right time." She took Kirby's handkerchief and held it over his wound in an effort to stop the bleeding.

Kirby's mind went back to the times he had heard his dad say the same thing from the pulpit: *how often do the bad times turn out to be exactly what we need?*

In a few minutes, policemen were swarming the Rittman property. Kirby was loaded into an ambulance headed toward Floyd County Medical Center where he got to spend the night before being released the following day. Both Judson and Sheila were taken away in handcuffs by the police. Sheila refused to talk with anyone. She still had not uttered a word when they were loaded in the back seat of a police cruiser, but no one there missed the stare she gave Connie.

CHAPTER 24

"What a great day for a cookout. A Saturday with perfect weather," Amos told his wife when she brought him more burgers to be grilled.

"And a great turnout," Carol declared, shifting to view more than thirty of their friends buzzing about the yard, engaged in activities ranging from volleyball to small group conversation.

Amos and Carol, along with Riley, were in their glory, preparing the food with the help of several other people. Kirby was on crutches, but nothing he couldn't handle. It was an old-fashioned summer cookout in good old Adairsville, Georgia. *It doesn't get any better than this,* Amos decided when he turned over a burger. No one called it a celebration, but for Amos, that's exactly what it was. Kirby was home from the hospital. His wound was healing. The cloud that had been hanging over them, the unsolved murder of James, was lifted, and the killer was behind bars. It looked as if future leadership for the Gordan businesses would soon be in place. That for which they had been praying, Kirby's spiritual life, was perhaps the biggest item they had to celebrate. Earlier in the day Kirby gave them some exciting news about his plans. *It's a good day to be alive,* Amos told himself.

When Kirby saw Charley Nelson and his wife Tonya arrive, he hobbled over to where the couple were taking some food from their car. "Hey Chief. Welcome to the Gordan/Edwards compound. I'm glad you two could make it. Could I borrow you for a few minutes?"

"Is that okay, honey?" Charley asked his wife.

"You do what you like. I'm going over there to spend a little time with the Morgan baby."

"She has a special reason to be interested in babies," Charley told his friend on crutches.

"Don't tell me you two are expecting?" Kirby asked.

"That's what I'm telling you," he answered. "It'll be our first."

"Congratulations," Kirby called out to Tonya as she walked away from them.

"Charley never could keep a secret," Tonya answered, waving without looking back.

"Let's go to the study where we can talk without interruption," Kirby suggested.

"I think I've put most of the pieces together, but I'd like to hear from you the complete run down of the facts concerning Uncle James's murder," Kirby told Charley as they were making their way to their destination.

"Well, you're family. Since you and Riley are his closest remaining relatives, you have the right to hear the whole story, and besides, you're the guy who took the bullet." Charley paused when they walked into the study. "This is one of the most beautiful man-made places on Earth," he remarked, staring at the Good Shepherd window. "I was here once before, and I didn't want to leave."

"I know what you mean. I sometimes think Uncle James designed this spot and willed it to me to help me deal with my spiritual doubts. That's just the sort of thing he would do. And you know what? It's working—that, along with Riley and Amos. I've got a long way to go, but I'm starting to get on solid ground. Have you gotten Judson and Sheila to talk?" Kirby asked.

"As far as I know, Sheila still hasn't spoken a word since the arrest. She just sits around staring into space. But I did get Judson to talk by telling him that if he would tell me the whole story, we could make sure his daughter gets the help she needs. He opened up and everything he told us seems to fit."

"So, you think he was being completely truthful?" Kirby asked.

"I think he was. He said with the note coming due, he called James, asking him to come out to his place so they could talk about it. When James got there, he was repairing some plumbing in one of the bathrooms. He said he came into the hall to answer the doorbell with a large pipe wrench in his hand. He laid it on a table that sits beside the door to let James in. They went on into the sitting room where they talked business. Judson told him about the deal he had cooking involving the very property in question. He informed him that he could not pay him what he owed him on the date stated on the note, but if he could be patient for a couple more months till the sale would be finalized, he would have plenty of money to repay him with extra interest. According to him, James gave him his usual stern lecture about the importance of keeping one's word and being honest in business. He said he knew ultimately James would come around and give him more time. They had been through all this before with other deals. He knew that the lecture was just part of the process.

"He said he saw Sheila come from the hall to the doorway to the room they were in. She stood and listened to James's lecture. While he was still talking, she briefly left to return with the pipe wrench he had used earlier. Judson said he saw the wrench in her hand, but until she came up behind Mr. Gordan's chair and brought it down hard on his head, he had no idea why she had picked it up."

"Why would she do such a thing?" Kirby asked.

"That's the very question I asked him. His answer was diminished mental capacity. He said she had become more and more fixated on the good life with trips to Europe and such. She didn't understand Mr. Gordan's way. She didn't know that after all his ranting that he would come around. As far as she was concerned, he was about to pull the rug out from under them. So, she killed him.

"Judson told me that when they checked and found James dead, he didn't know what to do. How could he send his daughter to live the rest of her life in prison? After thinking about it for a while, he called an old friend from Jasper who owed him a couple of favors. That friend agreed to meet him at his home in two hours. That was the man who helped him push James's car into the ravine. Incidentally, we arrested that man yesterday afternoon. He's safely locked away in the Bartow County Jail."

"Okay, I follow you up to this point, but what about the break-in here in this study, and the shot taken at Connie? Then later the break-in at Connie's home?" Kirby asked. "That had to be Rittman. What prompted those?"

"The day James was killed, they searched his pockets, looking for the note, but he obviously didn't have it on him. They didn't think much about that until several weeks later when they began to hear rumors, most likely initiated by one or more of my officers, that we were not investigating James's death as an accident but rather a homicide. They knew if the note was found, it could appear to be a motive. Judson knew this room was James's favorite workplace. Most likely the note would be somewhere here. That's why he broke in. Obviously, he didn't find it here, but he did find those file folders lying on the desk. A quick glance at one of them revealed that his grandfather was being implicated in the death of a government man. Seems his grandfather made a lot of his money as a bootlegger. Being the proud man he is, Judson wasn't going to let that information get out, so he picked up that folder. Before he left, he decided to take them all, so as not to give a hint to his identity. If someone deciphered which folder was missing, he would, no doubt, be the top suspect, but with all of them gone, there was no such problem."

"That makes a lot of sense. But why did he shoot at Connie or her mother in the park?"

"He told me that James informed him that he had not told Amos about the note because he knew he would disapprove. He thought the only other person who might have knowledge of the deal was Connie, since she did some of his paperwork. The idea was to eliminate the only person who might be able to reveal this menacing information. Judson said he was so nervous when he took the shot that he doubted he could have hit the side of his barn. He said he later determined he missed because psychologically he just couldn't do it. When he broke into Connie's garage, according to him, it wasn't that her car was missing that caused him to leave. He said he didn't know which car was hers. He got that far and decided he couldn't go through with it and left."

"I don't know if I believe that or not. I'll have to mull that over, but I guess it doesn't matter. There's enough here to keep him in prison for a while," Kirby suggested.

"You bet there is," Charley responded. "You might also want to know about the business with the van and then Connie being taken by Sheila. I can see Judson's point about diminished mental capacity when I consider closely this part of the story. It appears Sheila really had it bad for you, probably because of your inheritance."

"Of course it was my inheritance that drew her to me. I guess you figured it couldn't have been my charm," Kirby drolly reacted.

"When she saw Connie with you at church and maybe other places, she blew a gasket," Charley continued. "She took explosives from one of the outbuildings. They were left over from a supply that was used to remove stumps or some such farm project. She blew up the van out of pure spite. The man seen in the parking lot was indeed Judson. He was there trying to find Sheila to prevent her from harming herself or someone else."

"And what about her taking Connie at gunpoint?" Kirby asked.

"Same reason," Charley told him. "Spite! Maybe she thought she would eliminate competition. It's possible she would have killed Connie if things had turned out differently."

"It's hard to believe that anyone could be that mentally deranged, but I guess it happens," Kirby acknowledged. "We'd better get back to the picnic before someone like your wife sends out a search party for us."

"Will you be going back to Florida soon or will you stay with us awhile longer?" Charley asked Kirby as they were walking back to the heart of activity.

"I talked with my chief down there yesterday. I told him it was going to be about three months before I'll be able to use this leg normally. He suggested I take a leave of absence for those three months rather than returning there to sit behind a desk. In the meantime, I can decide whether I want to go back. I might opt to stay here and run the businesses with which I've been entrusted, but I will miss law enforcement if I choose to do that."

"Perhaps, for a time, you could do some police work as well as run your businesses. There are times when I could use a consultant, even one limited to one leg. You interested?"

"You'd better believe I am, but does anything ever happen around here that would require my services?" Kirby asked, before laughing.

Riley was walking from the kitchen area, carrying several items of food. Mike was all smiles beside her with his own load. After delivering their supplies, Mike returned to the kitchen for more. "I thought you were going to talk with Mike, sis," Kirby rather solemnly said.

"Yes Pa, I did. He asked me if it was okay for him to hang around anyway. He suggested he wanted to be nearby if I changed my mind. I told him I had no problem with that if he fully understood that there's no room in my life for a serious relationship at this time. He said he understood. We agreed we would continue to be good friends for now. He said being good friends with someone as beautiful, charming, and fun as me was better than nothing. How do you chase someone like that away?" she asked.

"So, nothing has changed," Kirby concluded.

"I don't know. Maybe it hasn't, but it's all good anyway," she told him.

"Maybe so, princess, maybe so," he said, kissing her on the cheek.

Kirby looked for Connie. She hadn't arrived when he went into the study with Charley. Surely, she was here by now. He found her on the swing in the garden. He came up behind her to start gently pushing her. She looked back and smiled. "I was wondering where the crippled boy was. How's the leg?" she asked.

"The leg feels fine. It just doesn't function as it should, but it will soon."

"I hear you're going to stay with us for at least another three months," she stated.

"That's right. Is that good news or bad news?"

"I'll have to think about that for a while," she said, and then quickly followed with, "I've thought about it and it's good news."

"I was hoping it would be. And what about you? Have you decided about that job you were offered? Are you going to take it?"

"I have to," she told him.

"Why do you have to?"

"I have to because someone must be around to protect the boss against all the girls stalking him."

"You're never going to let me live that down, are you?" Kirby asked.

"I don't plan to," she answered.

Kirby caught her when the swing came back. She turned her head toward him. Their mouths met for a sweet kiss.

Five little children, The Cleaning Crew children and two others, standing nearby clapped as they laughed and then put their hands over their eyes.

AFTERWORD

Adairsville, Georgia first came to the attention of mystery readers in the four-volume Davis Morgan Mystery Series. Upon conclusion of that series, some of our fans strongly suggested the new series also be set in the quaint little North Georgia town. So here we are, back in the town where serious crime occurs much more often in our books than in real life. If you are a Davis Morgan reader, you noticed some of the people from that series got brief exposure in this, the first Adairsville Heritage Mystery Series title. After all, it's a small town.

We hope you like the new characters: Kirby, Riley, Connie, Amos, Carol, and the gang as much as we do. It's going to be fun watching them pull it together. The title of this volume came mostly from Kirby's quest for spiritual stability that will continue to be a work in progress throughout the series. Most likely, you noticed Kirby's response to the story of the Pine Log campground earthquake. Perhaps you would be interested in knowing it's a true story marked by a sign on the grounds of the historical campground. Go by sometime and look. Occasionally, inserting a historical fact, and of course area landmarks, is what makes using the town we so love as the setting for our stories so much fun.

Yes, the *Solid Ground* mystery is solved. We now know who murdered Uncle James, but there are so many other questions left hanging. What about the Kirby/Connie romance? Does it have a chance to blossom into true love? Will Riley make it to law school, and will she find love? Is there more of Amos and Carol's past still to come to light? We'll get the answers to those questions and others while following Kirby and Riley through future probes of fascinating mysteries straight from the annals of little Adairsville, Georgia.

Danny & Wanda Pelfrey
Adairsville, Georgia